Prais

"Aly l story
writ ıe into
her (stories
that ll look
easy ıibited
cele

ɽRETT

"*Gr* s about
ang drawn
cha mb the
dep ; while
sin ıetry, a
prc world-
soa

RTONE

Graveyard of the Atlantic

OTHER BOOKS BY ALYSON HAGY

Hardware River
Madonna on Her Back
Keeneland

Graveyard of the Atlantic

SHORT STORIES BY

Alyson Hagy

Graywolf Press
SAINT PAUL, MINNESOTA

Publication of this volume is made possible in part by a grant provided by the Minnesota State Arts Board through an appropriation by the Minnesota State Legislature, and by a grant from the National Endowment for the Arts. Significant support has also been provided by the Bush Foundation; Dayton's, Mervyn's, and Target stores through the Dayton Hudson Foundation; the McKnight Foundation; and other generous contributions from foundations, corporations, and individuals. To these organizations and individuals we offer our heartfelt thanks.

Published by Graywolf Press
2402 University Avenue, Suite 203
Saint Paul, Minnesota 55114

www.graywolfpress.org

Published in the United States of America

ISBN 1-55597-301-9

2 4 6 8 9 7 5 3 1
First Graywolf Printing, 2000

Library of Congress Catalog Card Number: 99-067242

Cover Design and Map: Nora Koch

Contents

Acknowledgments

Thank you to the editors who included the following stories in their publications: “Sharking,” *Virginia Quarterly Review;* “The Snake Hunters,” the *Chicago Tribune,* as part of the Nelson Algren Awards; “North of Fear, South of Kill Devil,” *Shenandoah;* “Graveyard of the Atlantic,” *Mississippi Review,* as a finalist for the *Mississippi Review* Prize; “Semper Paratus,” *Five Points;* “Brother, Unadorned,” *Passages North;* “Search Bay,” *Ploughshares* and *Best American Short Stories 1997.*

I’m also indebted to *Ribbon of Sand* by John Alexander and James Lazell for its information on king snakes.

Good friends helped me launch this vessel. Thanks to Mandy Hoy for her sandy encouragement, Beth Haas and Joel Lovell for their sharp eyes at Old Town, Michael Paterniti and Sara Corbett for egging me on, Greg Netzer for cheering with microbrews, Janet Holmes for her wisdom, David Romtvedt and Mark Jenkins for asking the hard questions, Kim Kafka for her warm meals and warmer heart, and Bruce and Raven Wallace for showing me the true Search Bay.

In memory of Edwin L. "Pop" Williams
who showed us the islands

For RWS, fisher of water and words

What is a man who has no landscape?
Nothing but mirrors and tides.

ANNE MICHAELS

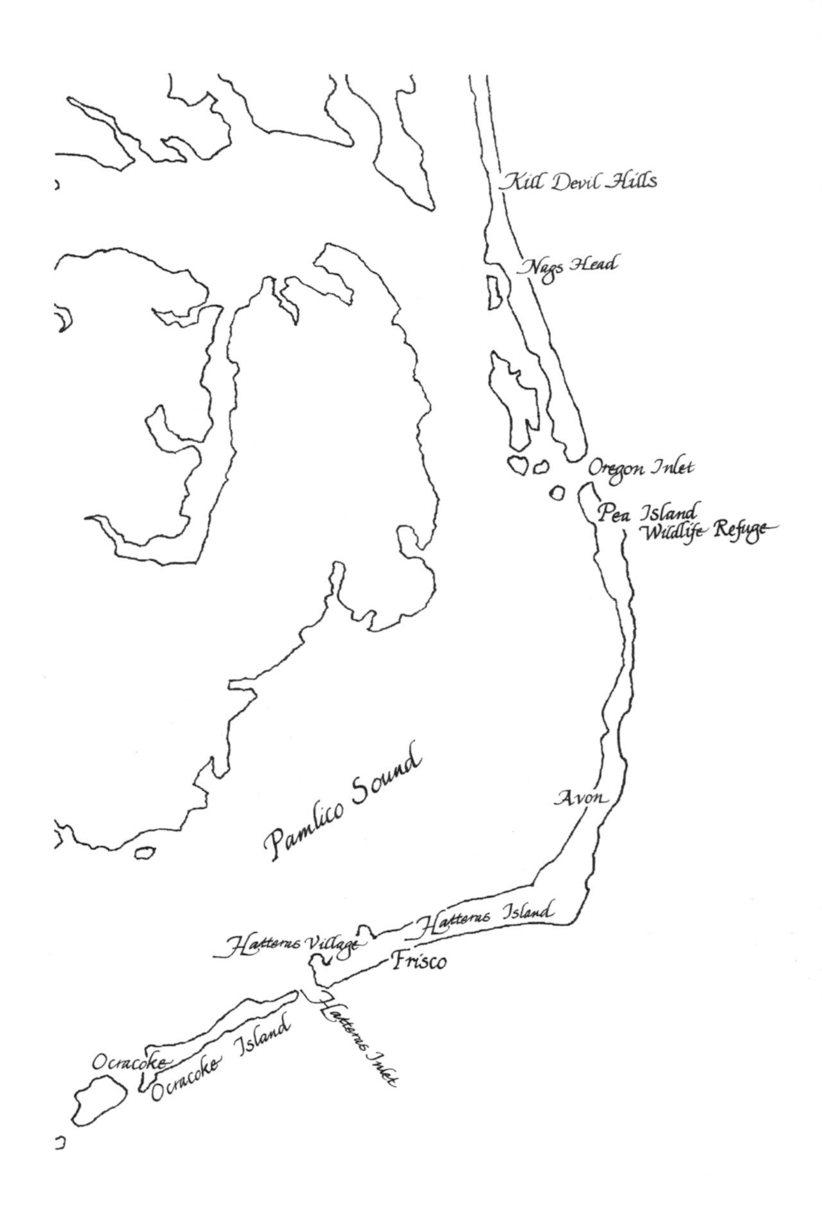
Kill Devil Hills
Nags Head
Oregon Inlet
Pea Island
Wildlife Refuge
Pamlico Sound
Avon
Hatteras Island
Hatteras Village
Frisco
Hatteras Inlet
Ocracoke
Ocracoke Island

Graveyard of the Atlantic

Sharking

I know some fellows who believe fishing is more than recreation and more than a bad habit. I even know a dozen stand-up guys who'd rather drop line in a mud puddle than play eighteen holes at Pebble Beach. Soulmates, those guys. But I've never been one to claim fishing is the be-all and end-all. I've got a grown daughter married to a chief petty officer up in Norfolk; she and her kids are worth the sunrise to me. And the love of a woman—I mean the real skingrain kind of love—that's surely the blood equal of solitude on the water. When I drive down to the pier with my coolers and my gear and my all-night shark-radar mood, however, I don't care to be interrupted.

Now that I'm retired, I go for shark maybe thirty times a year. Big Al was the one who got me to tally my excursions; he's damn competitive that way. Still, the days when I seriously counted brook trout and salmon and tequila shots and hard-ons are pretty much behind me. It doesn't make sense to apply that kind of bullshit to snagging sharks. Sharking is primarily attitude. Like climbing a mountain to meet one of those mysterious lama monks, something like that. You got your rituals, you keep to yourself. Sometimes you hook a beauty, but mostly, almost always, you don't.

Frankie, the guy who's running Frisco Pier this season, is good about my quirks. I pay my four dollars just like everybody else only I stay out all night, even after he shuts down at two, and that's fine with him. I've never had any trouble with the help here—they're ex-navy lots of times, or ex-cons, sometimes just ex-schoolteachers happy to bum around again like they did when they were eighteen. Frankie is solid, and he'll make change for the cigarette machine if you want it. He knows I'm good for free beer, too, which pleases him since he doesn't like to sneak it from the snack bar.

On a weeknight I'm pretty much guaranteed my spot at the end of the pier, just past the utility shed. Tourists beat me there on occasion, but they don't stay. They get restless if a fish doesn't latch onto their bait after about ten minutes. Besides, Frankie tells them their luck will be better midpier where the surf begins to break, which is mostly true. He knows I like my elbow room. He also knows I'll get it—at the southern corner, best place to keep my line clear—one way or another.

I can be downright gentlemanly once my bait's in the water and the sky's gone dark and hovering. But I'm a big man, wide enough to cover the top of a Coleman cooler with one haunch. The beard, the black cap, and the smeary Indonesian tattoos give some tourists the idea I might be a biker, so they sidle clear. Others, especially those whiny-type dads trying to teach their sons to fish, they got something else to prove, some need to hang out over the everlasting end of the pier like they're Columbus on the edge of the world. So they get too close to the rods I set up to catch my bait, they tangle their lines with mine, then swear at themselves or wise-eye me like I'm some bum on a park bench. In either case, they pretty quickly leave. Sometimes because of the bowie knife I pull to cut the tangled lines. Sometimes because the babble I produce as I hunker down on my cooler, a beer in each hand, doesn't dovetail with their idea of a family vacation.

So I aim for a perfect evening. A Tuesday in early May, three weeks before the tourist season cranks up. Wind out of the north, five to ten knots. Clear sky, and Big Al is nowhere in sight. Chances are he's on the pier at Nags Head because he's a lazy coot who won't steer his ass another hour south to Hatteras Island to take me on. Am I complaining? I am not. The night's a joke when we're both rigging floats, swapping tales about the mako the charters have brought in, or the hammerheads the surfers have skedaddled from. I don't like how I get sucked into it, verbal sparring of the lowest, toothiest sort, but it's a weakness of mine. One of several.

Besides the folks on the beach, the only company I've got is fifty yards back where a lanky, careful-moving couple in bill caps and dark green work clothes are bottom-fishing with cut mullet. I like their looks. They've each got a tackle box, they hardly speak a word, their eyes are focused on the scalloped water of the middle distance. The woman's had a good day; I saw her bagging fillets when I passed by. The man, well, maybe he hasn't caught a damn thing, but I can tell by the set of his head that he'd never think of complaining. He might consider trying another spot tomorrow, or the day after, but he's too aware of his good fortune to bitch and moan. I like to see people inhabiting their fishing time like that—you know, living right in it. Gives me hope that the world may yet learn to leave us all alone.

I lay out the pieces of my rig like I'm a mechanic, or maybe a gourmet chef. The tide has shifted, but I've got an hour before I need to drop my float and there are preparations to be savored. The hook—a six-inch single barb—and the three-foot steel leader are old, though you wouldn't know that by looking. I keep things polished. I got one white garbage bag, a spool of catgut thread, 800 yards of 80-pound test on a top-of-the-line Daiwa reel, and my best St. Croix rod. The St. Croix's short and thick around as a longshoreman's thumb, looks more like an instrument of punishment than anything else. In my second-string cooler I've got a four-day-old amberjack, stinkingest piece of bait I've had all season.

So I'm at it, a heavy man working light on his feet. Stuff laid out on a pair of striped bath towels, each thing in its place. I re-oil the reel. I finger the leader for chinks or flaws. I back off and crack open a beer just so I don't rush. That's when I see her, a wisp of a woman clearing the glare of the halogen lights posted every twenty yards or so. She's got a bucket in one hand, rod in the other. She's walking that slow, self-absorbed walk, heel to toe, no hip swing, and I see exactly how it's going to be. She's going to set up in my outpost, right on my sea-splashed fang of a world, and I'm going to have to deal with it.

She stops short when she sees me, takes in the clutter of my passion and flattens her lips. In her forties, I'd guess. Too thin for my taste, but dressed practically in a yellow shirt, jeans, a pair of boys' tennis shoes. Got a blue windbreaker knotted around her waist and a bandanna on her head. She looks me in the eye just once to be polite, then threads her way around my stuff to set up in the northern corner. I can't figure right off what she's after—puppy drum, maybe—but it's clear she'll stay out of my way. I peg her as one of those edgy divorced types who like to see if they can hack loneliness in the dark.

I get back to business. Rig the pole, check the wind, blow the garbage bag up like it's a balloon and tie it off with catgut. Then the best part—lifting that vile jack from the cooler and running the hook through its gristly eyes. My homemade float will carry that sucker out with the tide a couple hundred yards before the catgut melts and drops the bait in deep water. And there she'll lay, grand and sour and available.

The waiting is the heart of it, of course. My companion knows that. She baits her own hook deliberately and without distraction. She never even looks at me, barely nods at the sightseers who wander out after their seafood and wine dinners in the village. Out of respect for her concentration, I don't holler when I drop my masterpiece over the rail. I just roam back to my cooler, spritz open a cold one, and take a gander at the stars, which make me think of the pale sky over Okinawa, which leads me to consider the slow fade-out of my marriage. No regrets. The wife and I both wrung what we could from twenty-five hopscotch years in the navy. Then she bailed to live with her sister in West Virginia. I see our daughter and grandkids more often than she does, but I'm not fool enough to think that makes me a better person.

I wonder if my lone friend in the corner has children. I watch her for a few minutes—my float is finally out of sight in the black draw of wind and water—and I make guesses at her life. No rings on her fingers that I can see, so I decide there's an asshole left behind in a good brick house somewhere, a drinker maybe, middle-aged guy scared of his own life. She's a fine person, I decide that too, though I can't quite say why she gets my vote. Then I notice the bandanna, how it folds and flips in the breeze, how it reveals uneven tufts of downy hair all over the back of her skull, and I rethink her history with the knowledge that the score has been less in her favor all along.

She's dyed that brave hair platinum blond, bless her, a fact that nearly makes me laugh. Skinny, sick, a stubborn sense of humor—I reckon she deserves a night like this, with the timbers shivering under her feet and the wind singing off the guide wires. All the nights she wants. I watch her lean into the chest-high rail as her bait does a free fall. When she sets the line, her shoulders and back relax, and I see her hips begin to sway. One, two, three. One, two, three. It's a thing I haven't noticed before. How the rhythm of the surf beneath us, the way she hears it, has her waltzing above the waves.

Seeing this makes me restless, so I stand to check my line, which doesn't need to be checked. I'm wondering how I'd be doing in the Texas hold 'em poker game at Eddie's in Virginia Beach, when I hear a commotion on shore. Hell. One look tells me all I need to know. Four or five guys have piled up a bonfire and are set to create some mayhem. I can tell they're drunk by the hee-haw quality of their laughter. Their faces are like orangish half-moons from this distance, staggering planets around a sparking sun. No problem. I'll tune them out. Which I do until a crescendo of shouting causes me to take another look. By God, I get acid in my throat then. The punks are muscling an inflatable raft into the surf, two guys clinging to the sides, and I know they're planning to row some bait into my territory and poach on my shark.

If I'm lucky, they'll capsize before they clear the surf. If I'm unlucky, they'll get out there and cross my line and cause big trouble for all of us. I grab the gut-smeared rail and shake it with my hands, wishing I had a rifle so I could pop a hole in that oversized doughnut of a raft. I don't quite swear out loud, but I hear a rattling scrape behind me and sense the woman looking at me, at my quivering temper, wondering why I'm suddenly so out of whack. She's right. *You're right,* I think. Where's my God damn poise and equilibrium?

I don't like how I feel—flummoxed, out-maneuvered—but I manage to let go of the rail.

Enough time passes for me to get halfway through a cheddar cheese and mustard sandwich. Then I hear a sound that doubles the coils in my guts and takes me back fifteen years, to when a steam pipe blew on the supply ship I was assigned to and scalded the unlucky sods working nearby. Deep pain and panic. I can't see much, just a couple of dark figures zigzagging from that bonfire to the surf, but I assume the worst. The idiot raft has gone over in the waves.

I'm down the pier in half a minute, over the rail by the snack bar before Frankie has even gotten out the door. "Call Leon right now," I say. "Get him up here." Frankie's face is thick with sleep and confusion, but he understands the important part. Two deputies with lifesaving equipment can be here in three minutes, and we might need them.

I pump my legs through sand. The first guy, arms straight out in front of him, rushes up to meet me like I'm a long-lost cousin. He's wet to the waist and shivering, though not from cold. The second guy comes in behind me like he's been up to the parking lot or something, looking for help that isn't there. They're both hopping from foot to foot, saying something about Wayne and Talbot and the raft, though it's all coming out in hoarse fragments that don't help me a bit. I don't know what I'm going to do, of course. I'm overweight and don't swim that well, regardless of my years on the pitching decks of the U.S.N. I take it as a good sign that I'm absorbing a lot of detail with Kodak-type clarity, like the fact these fellows are both wearing shirts from the University of Tennessee, though it's hard not to connect those neon orange shirts to the general stupidity of the situation.

We all three trot into the surf up to our knees. There's some shouting coming from beyond the white fringe of the breakers, but it's impossible to tell how desperate it is. The story I've got by now is that Wayne and his brother were in the raft. Then Talbot, who was fishing from shore, hooked something big and heavy, a thing he swore was a shark, and the boys rowed over to see what it was. That's when the yelling started. Maybe the raft capsized, maybe it didn't. All they know is that Wayne and his brother, who doesn't appear to have a name of his own, are wearing life jackets and both know how to swim. Talbot, who is drunk enough to worry even these two locos, decided to follow his fishing line to the source of the trouble. According to the report I'm getting, Talbot's never soaked himself in anything bigger than a bathtub.

God almighty. The first thing I say is, Boys, maybe it's best we wait for the law. Your friends will be washing up around our ankles any minute.

Second thing I say is, Do you have a flashlight?

They do. Talbot's got one with him too, though he apparently hasn't managed to turn it on. I assess the situation one more time. The surf's not *that* rough, but the current is strong. I turn on the light and, guessing at the raft's drift, hightail it down the beach about two hundred yards. One Tennessee guy stays near the bonfire to flag down Leon when he arrives; the other one follows me like a duckling after its nettled mother.

Of course I'm a hard-hearted SOB, so I still manage to think about my bait and how it's lying out there unattended, how my night's a ruin. These fellows have trifled with the ocean and with me—the way I see it, they've only got one strike left. I wade in, waves smacking at my thighs and chest. I haven't been in salt water this deep since I slipped off a dock in the Philippines, many, many whiskeys ago. Go from sandbar to sandbar, I tell myself, keep your own damn head above water while you try to pinpoint that raft.

They find *me,* of course. Two ratty-looking boys in life jackets, their long rock'n'roll hair plastered to their foreheads and necks. One of them's got a cut-up arm, but they're safe, been trying to swim the raft in against the tide, which hasn't been easy. They look surprised as hell to see me, and hangdog grateful. What about Talbot, I ask, shouting into the wind that's picked up again, where is he? The brothers look befuddled, then a little weepy. The one I think of as Wayne, who looks most likely to have that name even in his present condition, stops dog-paddling with his free hand and grabs at the front of my shirt. Tells me I must be crazy, mistaken. There's only them two with the raft. Talbot would never come out yonder, he says. He don't know how to swim.

By now Mr. Tennessee Shirt Number One has joined us and we're set to drag that raft to dry land. Or we will be, once the Three Musketeers stop spitting and slapping fives. Talbot, they pant. Talbot, man, we got to find him. I can see a wheel of lights beyond the pier now, the tiny lighthouse flashes of the rescue van. We may get lucky, I think to myself, and be out one drunk fisherman instead of three. Tugging on the raft is going to flare up the bursitis in my left shoulder, I'm thinking that too, when Mr. Tennessee Shirt who's stumbling beside me says, What if a shark got hold of Talbot after he got hold of it? He looks behind him as he says this, then back at me with eyes the size of line spools. He wants me to tell him it can't be so.

I ask the soggy brothers, Did you all see what Talbot had on his line? No, Wayne says, they never got that far, a breaker flipped them. His brother, who has got the cut arm and a mustache with maybe five hairs in it, appears relieved they missed their chance. Probably hooked a lunker drum, I say. Naw, says Tennessee Shirt, no way. The drag was set tight and the line played on out. Whatever he had was damn big. Tennessee's hands fly off the raft to measure just how big and his eyes are filled with braggart's pride for his buddy until he remembers why he's staggering through the strongest undertow on the Atlantic coast, losing his shoes to the devil's kiss of the tide. Then it's like the bones in his long hillbilly neck have collapsed and his chin's at his chest in prayer or cruel sobriety, I can't tell which.

Don't worry, boys, I say. He probably just snagged one of them Nazi subs sunk offshore during the war. It won't harm him none.

Wayne snorts and sticks out his jawbone so I'll know he gets the joke. I have less luck with his brother, who practically crawls back into the raft to get his legs out of the thundering, ghostly water. My main point is well-taken though: We can't do toot for Talbot until we get our own selves back to land.

Ten minutes of coughing and dunking and we're in. Frankie's Jeep is working its way down the beach while Leon sweeps the water with a portable searchlight. I can't help but notice how much that light resembles the Atlantic moon, slightly bluish, slightly creamy, when it sails across these same sands on a silent night. The pier's gone dark too, though I can't figure why Frankie thought dousing the lights would be a help. All I know is I'm sorry I'm not up there playing captain on my black skeleton of a ship. I don't look forward to what Frankie and Leon are going to find.

The Jeep stops about 500 yards south of where I've fallen to my knees. I spit and wheeze salt water into my beard, allowing myself a cuss or two in honor of lost stamina and lost youth. The other three sound as whipped as I am but take off down the beach anyway. They've got to get to their buddy. I admire their dog-pack loyalty.

It's part of what got me through my six-month cruises in the Pacific. Part of what helps one man tolerate another.

By the time I limp my way to the scene, I find Leon in the posture I've anticipated, on his knees by the victim's swollen face, his movements hindered by his stiff, glowing vest and loaded equipment belt. Leon's a local boy who did four years with the Coast Guard in Oregon before getting on with the Dare County Sheriff. I know him because his dad runs a good charter boat. He looks at me, then flicks his serious eyes to a slick grayish lump behind him in the sand. God almighty.

Talbot caught himself a ray, a big one, and that's at the heart of this whole fiasco. Of course it takes a shitload of ignorance to mistake a ray for a shark, though I've seen it happen more than once, especially in daylight when a flapping wing looks like a dorsal fin to a tourist. I can just see the look on Talbot's face when his rod bent, him all wicked with drink and pride, just scared enough to get bullying. He thinks the only big, bad creatures in the sea are sharks—the dumb ass. I note he managed to foul-hook the poor thing as well, which is why Leon has brought it to my attention. I pull my knife and kneel by the ray's blunt, cowlike nose. Locate the hook by hand since it's buried on the underside of a wing, then cut it loose with a sizable chunk of rubbery flesh besides. Like most ocean critters, the ray can't make a sound, even in agony, and I'm halfway pleased about that. The noise coming from behind me—whispering, sobbing, the occasional chunk and clang of medical equipment—is plenty enough.

I ship the ray back out to sea, its five-foot span quickly buoyant in the fanning glitter of water. Tennessee Shirt Number One helps me—the ray must weigh near seventy pounds—and it's then he tells me that Talbot's still alive, passed out more from alcohol and fatigue than from water in his lungs. "They want to take him on up to the clinic in Nags Head," he says. "So I reckon they'll do that. We thank you for your help."

"You're welcome to it," I say, running my fingers through air until I realize my hat's missing, washed away during our crazy water dance. "Maybe do me a favor next time you all come down this way—" And I start to tell him to stick to trout fishing, for Chrissake, and leave the bigger game to wised-up, busted-up bastards like me. But I don't. I go back to the old rules. No judgment, no chitchat.

"Yes, sir," he says with good church manners, finishing my thought for me. And he thanks me again. I nod to Leon and his partner, who are lifting Talbot into the back of Frankie's Jeep. Old Talbot will puke in there, I'm sure of it, and Frankie will be mad as hell. It'll add an extra hoot to the story he'll be telling in the snack bar by lunchtime, however, which is worth the time it'll take him to scour his floor mats. Frankie loves his stories. I lumber off into the night as solo as can be, my body aching from skin to bone, and the last words I hear come from

Wayne's brother, who's asking Deputy Leon what he knows about them sneaky Nazi subs.

She's still there, by gosh, fishing with no more company than the milky starlight. I make out her yellow shirt the same time I make out the stripes on my towels, which are still flat on the pier under the weight of extra tackle and beer cans. I wonder if she's had any luck. I wonder if she knows what happened out there, beyond her ken. I wonder if she cares. Figure I'll ask her as much after I check my orphaned line, maybe bend the rules one last time and offer her a drink. So I lift my St. Croix from where it's nestled tight in its premium corner and . . . nothing. Line's been snapped clean off. I can feel the loose filament whipping back toward my mouth, my eyes.

"I heard it run," she says, her voice smooth with the lull of an accent I can't quite place. "Went real fast for five, ten seconds. I was worried you'd lose the rod."

But you didn't pick it up? This is the unforgiving question that breaks into my mind. I take a step or two toward her, the St. Croix in one fist, my other hand lost in the salty mat of my hair as it searches for my cap.

"I watched it for you," she says, turned around so she doesn't have to speak over the sharp ledge of her shoulder. "I did that, in the time I had." I see she's no longer waltzing, and I also see, or think I see, that she's younger than I first thought. Or maybe I get that from the lack of hair at her temples. She's not joking with me, though, and she's not shy. Her words are steadily matter-of-fact, just like I like them.

"Think I had a shark?"

One side of her mouth pulls tight, and I see dry wrinkles there, etched from worry and pain. "I think you had trouble, and I'm sorry."

"Yeah. Trouble." I lay my rod at my feet and turn away. It appears I had a rare chance and it didn't stay mine. She's knows there's not a damn thing you can say to a person about a time like that.

"Those fellows make out all right?" She's bent at the waist over her tackle box now, all dark legs and whispers.

"Guess so, fools that they are. They're alive."

"That's nice."

I stop wiping my face with a towel and focus on the woman again. She's standing straight, and her eyes are hard in a way I recognize. My daddy's eyes when he was rigid with angina. The eyes of a luckless yeoman crushed in a cargo bay.

She repeats herself. "That's nice. I'm glad." She wrestles every word until it comes out easy.

The world is night-watch black, and talk—even the sound of talk—is no good for either of us. I'm not going to save her from a damn thing. She's not going to ask anyone to try. I scrape into my corner, and she flips the bail on her reel and gets back to business. We stay that way a long while. It occurs to me that I'll probably never come out here without thinking of her, and knowing that is a strange sort of gift after the kind of night I've had. I'll be out here again, a hundred more times I hope, and somehow so will she, sketched darkly against land's end. Gone in body, held in memory, like we all might hope to be.

The Snake Hunters

Aaron looked out over Pamlico Sound, an automatic benediction. When he was a young child, and Grandpa and Shaw were still going for mullet, he played on that water's edge while they repaired their nets. Time seemed to pass easily then, his grandfather and uncle filling that time with habits honed from years of trial and argument. Grandpa gave directions, told tales, asked for lemonade or hard candy from the house. Shaw said little, but he didn't have to say much—the close-motion way he worked spoke for itself. Neither of them could be separated from the island or their history on it. *All we got out here is what we teach our hands,* Grandpa would say, eyeing the gray muscle of current that clenched at his skiff, *what's tight in these heads.*

Aaron slipped Shaw's old hammer into his belt, then stacked the scraps of two-by-six under his arm. Mrs. Austin's dock was as good as new. He'd earned his ten dollars. As he started down the breakwater toward

Grandpa's place on the other side of the point, Slag, Mrs. Austin's black Lab, limped along the broken stone ledge behind him. Years of fetching ducks in cold water had ruined the dog's hips. It was common knowledge that dogs went down fast on Ocracoke Island, just like the buildings and engines and TV antennas set out to sway in the rough salt air.

He paused on the tide-eaten slope of the point to shoo Slag back home. He could see the weathered face of Grandpa's house too well from there, the sunburnt fringe of weeds, the empty boat slips. He did what he had time for—mowed the front yard and kept the windows boarded, set a few mousetraps. The skiff, which belonged to him now, was tied up at his friend Shorty's. His mother had sold the other boats after Grandpa's last visit to the cancer doctor in Morehead City.

When he got to the boathouse, he dumped the wood near a sloppy pile of roofing shingles. The boathouse was still organized according to Shaw's rules of practical chaos. The neat racks of fishing rods and oiled reels were the only shrines to logic in the place; everything else was crammed into oyster crates or coffee cans. He'd never even bothered to close the top of Shaw's mammoth red toolbox, leaving it open after the accident because that's the way Shaw always left it, a habit that made Grandpa growl. Pulling the hammer from his belt, he dropped it onto the chunky scatter of sockets and screwdrivers. He would always wish his uncle had been more like his old self when he took that final trip into the

Gulf Stream, able to burn cigarette holes in the overdue bills, a rebel in the smallest, most ornery ways. Instead, Shaw had reckoned himself a last-ditch gambler and went on to lose everything in one black ocean game.

He locked the boathouse and pedaled to the highway, where he wove back and forth among the slowpoke cars fresh off the ferry from Swanquarter. Tourists were another matter. He did his best to ignore them except when he was selling T-shirts and snow cones at Vernon's roadside stand. Tourists were ghosts to him, clamoring shapes that appeared according to season and the weather. Other than his friends' loud interest in the summer girls who lollygagged on the beaches, most natives pretended to have little use for mainlanders. They claimed nothing from them but their cash.

He found Shorty sharing a cigarette with Lucas in Shorty's backyard. They were his oldest friends, close-coupled boys who talked as though their futures would be there when they looked for them. "Hey, bud," Shorty yelled, shadowboxing his way toward Aaron's chin. "We gotta load up and get to the campground. Ma's over at the store, so I'm loose."

"Sure," Aaron said, ducking low, "like any of those girls will pay attention to us."

"They like working men, just ask Lucas here how they eyeball him when he's washing down his daddy's boat. Girls like all that fish blood and sweat, don't they,

Lukey? How y'all muscle them dolphin and yellowfin up on the docks."

Lucas rolled his shoulders and laughed. "I know they hang around the older guys. Dooley's mate says he got laid last weekend by some skinny girl from up at New Jersey."

"All right." Shorty clapped his hands, then high-stepped toward his bike. "Y'all better hope there's enough to go around."

They saw the van right away. It was an old, tangerine-colored VW flanked by four worn canvas tents, an arrangement Shorty claimed meant girls or marijuana or both. Aaron wasn't so sure. He preferred the wide hem of the beach where his friends could do all of the talking while he fished. But Shorty believed he could seduce a mainland girl with nothing more than his Outer Banks accent; he never liked to let an opportunity pass. They could see a man tinkering with the van's engine. It wouldn't hurt to ask if he needed help, scout the situation that way.

The man was young and neatly bearded, his forehead striped white as though he usually wore a hat. He told the boys a fan belt had snapped; he was stranded at the campsite while the rest of his group explored the dunes to the north. They'd taken the other car.

Lucas spoke up. "You can replace that belt at the store in the village. It don't close till six."

"Sounds good," the man said. "I'm supposed to go down there to buy fish for dinner anyway. My students are boycotting my homemade beef stew."

That was all Lucas and Shorty needed to hear—the

guy was a teacher. It didn't matter that his accent was pure Carolina, his smile genuine enough. Fellows like this one, organized and confident, were too much like Mr. Singleton, the principal at Ocracoke School. They began popping restless wheelies on the pavement.

Something held Aaron stationary, however. Kept him from hunching over his taped handlebars and huffing toward the beach. Just a way to be weird, he thought, since all he really wanted to do was fish. He offered the man his bike.

"It's not so great." He tried not to blush at his rash surge of generosity. "It'll get you down there though. And Mr. George or one of the men at the dock can wrap your fish so you can haul it on the back."

"All right," the man said, extending a lightly freckled hand. "I'm David Pryor, by the way. I'll be as quick as I can."

"Don't worry about me." He slung an arm toward the ramp his buddies had already crossed. "I'm not in that kind of hurry."

"Well, thanks."

"Yeah, you too." He felt it punch him hard in the stomach then, the awkwardness he'd expected before. So he offered his name as a sort of anchor, a way to stop the drift. "Aaron Ballance," he said. "I'm Aaron."

The fishing was lousy, so he quit when the mosquitoes got bad. At the campsite he found even more mosquitoes and the sort of crazy festival air he didn't expect from a school field trip. Four guys, all taller than he was, necks lashed with sunburn, jeans and shoes streaked with mud, were gathered in a circle around David Pryor, drinking from plastic water bottles and gesturing wildly. They seemed to be telling a half-dozen stories at once; at every outburst of laughter their circle became smaller. He decided to grab his bike and get the hell out of there, but David saw him, and he was caught—sucked into a whirlpool of noisy, inattentive strangers.

The private hooting and jeering stopped long enough for introductions. Aaron matched names with faces as quickly as he could, holding the others' eyes until he'd tapped their moods. Jed was tall and heavy and pale, his blondish hair peaked in sweaty cowlicks above his ears, his light-colored eyes noncommittal. Finn was wiry and small, more like an island boy in build but far too fidgety to be local. He also wore thick glasses. Stevie was plump in the face, probably younger than the other two, and less obviously watchful of strangers. Aaron noticed how Stevie stood closest to David, as if he was in need of reassurance. The fourth person was not a boy at all, but a sunbaked, frizzy-haired older man whose clothes and elastic posture had made him momentarily indistinguishable from the group. David introduced him as Dr. Oskar, "the brains behind the operation," a tag that drew more laughter from the others.

"Yeah, Dr. Brains," Finn blurted, "why don't you tell

Aaron here how a Harvard guy's so smart he can't find one single snake on this stinking sandbar?"

"It's true. The child help I have is too busy complaining about wet feet and a few biting flies. I have no luck."

The voice was foreign-flavored, thickened by the doctor's good humor. But even though Dr. Oskar's arms were as long and muscled as a waterman's, Aaron could tell these guys—these men—came from another world. He shuffled his feet in the trampled sand, wondering where his bike was. David gave him a pinched smile, then stepped back to create an escape hatch into the fading afternoon. His bicycle leaned against the rear bumper of the van.

"You're welcome to stay for dinner, you know. We're not as scary as we sound, just excited about being on the island again. Cobia steaks and potatoes. It's on the house."

He shook his head, wanting to wish this David Pryor good luck but not knowing how to do it. So he was done, the last glance broken, when someone emerged from the nearest tent. It was a girl, small and white-legged in clean shorts.

"Oh." She finished tightening a red plastic belt and gave him a cockeyed grin. "Oh. Stop him, David. He lives here, right? I've got a million questions."

Pryor gave a one-sided shrug. "Aaron's about to leave. We haven't charmed him much, I'm afraid."

The girl was suddenly right in front of the bike, holding out a hand, two hands, and finally blocking his retreat with such a display of comic pleading he had to stop. He tried to look at her, maybe slough her off with a quick shrug, but there was too much energy in her eyes, too much demand. It was like being trapped in a spotlight.

"We're trying to catch snakes," she said. "I mean we *are* catching snakes, lots of them, but not the kind we want. Brown ones. Beautiful."

"Cottonmouths?" He caught his breath. He could hardly imagine this twig of a girl provoking a moccasin.

"No, no, no. Not those. *Lampropeltis getulus sticticeps.* A king snake. But not the regular black kind. This baby is brown, or like mahogany say, with ivory spots. Rare. Nearly extinct."

David interrupted, laying a hand on the back of the girl's neck. "Zara's pretty passionate about this," he laughed. "And a little relentless. But it's true you could be a good resource, along with some of the old timers, folks who know the topography. The Fish and Wildlife people are just as stumped as we are on this one. *Sticticeps* hasn't been seen in a long time."

"So what do you say?" To his astonishment the girl, this Zara, elbowed him in the ribs. A huge silver earring shimmered below one of her ears. "Help us out. Show us the secrets of the island." He could only hope he didn't look as dizzy as he felt. The lack of inhibition, the lemony scent of her short, dark hair—it all billowed about him like mainsails in a breeze.

"Sure. Okay. I don't have to work tomorrow until late," he lied, trying not to think about his crab pots. "I mean if you really want me."

"We want you. God, we *need* you," Zara shrilled, throwing her arms in the air. "We've only got two days left."

He tried to preempt his mother, explaining how crabbing was slow because the water was cooler than it ought to be. She stood at the narrow steel sink and scraped at the burned, uneaten edges of their dinner, still dressed in the navy blue smock she wore to clean rooms at the Pony Island Motel.

"Trina says Shorty's doing good, best he ever has."

"Shorty lies to his mom all the time. She never sees his take either. You know that."

"So you say. I told Mr. Spence you could clean the pool Saturday morning. Five dollars."

He picked up his smeared fork, clenched it, put it back down. "I'm too busy. What about Eric? It's his parents' motel."

His mother turned to face him, the grayish lines between her nose and chin drawn tight. "Eric doesn't need the money."

"What we need around here is a lot more than money." He fixed her with hooded eyes, recalling for a sickening instant that this false, bull-like expression was his father's, but holding it nonetheless. He was pissed off and weary, they both were, standing hard against some force of the future they couldn't begin to define. They'd lost Shaw, then Grandpa. And they were waiting for his dad to call the shots, like families did, island families anyway, but his dad was running a channel dredge in Philadelphia, best work he could find, and he was nothing more than a mosquito whine on the phone. Shaking his head to clear it, Aaron pushed free of the table and stood to go outside. Thought he might take a walk along the creek behind the Howard's, look for that disappearing snake. How hard could such a thing be?

He slipped off the unpainted porch into the mallow dusk. He'd left his mom with the dishes, a thing he hated to do, but he didn't want to risk a truce. Not yet. She wouldn't let him join the snake hunt if she found out about it; she still had the power to do that. His mother stored much of what she had left in him, and he guessed maybe she had to, but it made him want to stay out of her way all the same. Shaw had named the new boat, the *Katie B.,* after his sister when she was still known to be loyal and quarrelsome and sly. What Aaron saw in her now was fatigue without humor, rage without relief. He wondered if the Zara girl from the mainland could ever become like that, reclusive, depleted, worn down by what she cared about. He kicked his way along the shadowy path toward the Howard's bothered by the conclusion he drew from his own question.

He was at the campsite by six-thirty, having eaten breakfast and changed his clothes three times. He ended up wearing his best jeans and a damaged shirt Vernon had given him for free, one that featured an off-center portrait of Blackbeard with a long, inky stain beneath the pirate's braids. After his dark walk along the creek, where he'd seen nothing but the planet rings of rising fish, he'd spent a good portion of the night recalling Grandpa's stories, culling them for any mention of snakes. Grandpa had taught him how to fish, how to tell one kind of waterfowl from another. He'd passed on an entire library of cold-ass facts in duck blinds and the syrupy backwaters of the marshes. Given that, Aaron figured there wasn't much about Ocracoke he didn't know, or couldn't puzzle out, if he just breathed and took hold of a few good memories.

But David Pryor took him down a notch right away, though he was nice about it. They were drinking briny coffee while the boys struggled out of their tents and limped to the bathrooms. Dr. Oskar had been on the beach since dawn, doing his t'ai chi before the swell of the tide. Zara, David said, would sleep until the last possible moment. She always did.

So David explained how he'd seen the only known specimen of *sticticeps,* the Outer Banks king snake, when he was visiting friends in Massachusetts. It was dead by then, no more than a fat, flaking coil in a museum jar, yet he'd been fascinated. A herpetologist had captured it on Ocracoke in the 1950s and speculated that it might represent clear and uncommonly swift species adaptation. This sort of adaptation was Dr. Oskar's specialty, in fact. He, David, was just a high school biology teacher who'd been visiting the Banks since he was a kid. Finding that snake seemed like the perfect quest, he said. A private mystery. The careful application of science to a landscape he loved.

He spoke in a manner both vague and encompassing, nothing like the clannish hectoring Aaron had grown up with. He wore his hat now, a baseball cap from U.N.C., and he looked refreshed, magnified. He said there was something to be learned from the world, no matter where you were on it. He said biologists rarely experienced complete failure, that frustration could be a kind of blindness. There was information to be gleaned from every empty den and abandoned nest, from each absence, David said. This was what field scientists thrived on. The leftovers. The increments.

So this was their third trip—the first with students—and they'd found no sign of the snake. Green snakes, racers, countless water snakes, moccasins, lizards; they'd caught everything else. Zara wanted to survey the island rodents, reasoning they'd find *sticticeps* once they identified its sources of food, but today would be another day of plain old snake wrangling. "Springer's Point, maybe. We have permission to go there. Or Old Hammock Road. Unless you have some ideas."

He didn't say a word. David had mentioned that both Jed and Zara planned to become researchers in college; they'd all read piles of books. His own idea of biology was breaking up a jellyfish in a scoop net and watching it swim off in a dozen directions. It wouldn't be long before they'd see him for what he was, a fifteen-year-old kid who didn't care for school, who hardly knew what the hell he *did* care for.

Breakfast was granola bars and Pepsi, though Zara, when she finally emerged, contented herself with a mug of sun-brewed tea. Seeing her through the cool screen of morning light made him doubly uncomfortable. She wasn't at all pretty, not with a wrinkled sun hat jammed down to the top of her eyebrows, naked ears folded outward. Her skin was sleep-blotched, her small-featured face grim and uncommunicative. In fact, David and Dr.Oskar were the only ones who actually spoke to him, so he was relieved when the group was divided into two crews. Dr. Oskar would take Jed and Finn to Springer's Point. The rest of them were sentenced to the blackroot muck of Old Hammock. David reminded them all that it was as important to know where *sticticeps* didn't live as where it did.

"If he's anywhere," Stevie said, rolling his bleary eyes.

"She's here." Zara pointed toward the sand at her feet. "Be smart about that, okay. Respect it."

Jed snorted. "You don't know that, Zara. You don't *know* anything. No facts."

Aaron watched Zara's marble-veined eyes burn, then flicker. "You're right," she said, looking at David instead. "All I've got is a *feeling*. And feelings don't matter." She removed her hat like she wanted to shake her hair loose even though it was cut too short for that. David froze, red-faced, and Aaron waited for a regular quarrel to break out. But the tension was dispelled by Dr. Oskar's announcement of an equipment check. A few minutes later he and Jed and Finn were gone.

Aaron couldn't remember the last time he'd been to Old Hammock. He and Grandpa had gigged for flounder near there a few times, but the nature path the Park Service put in made Grandpa skittish of a place so overrun with alien faces and habits. When the cancer really kicked in, they'd stayed on the water close to home, Grandpa leaning back in the skiff with his haunted eyes closed, and Old Hammock became a distant jungle, another piece of the island relinquished.

Oddly, they began the hunt with almost no direction from David. The face that had been so expressive when he talked about his plans looked puffy, almost stupid, as he announced his intention to search the ditches along the highway. Then he shambled off. "Snake catchers are born, not made," Zara said, turning her back on David and centering Aaron in a piercing squint. "You can yell if you need help." There were widemouth jars and preservatives and containers for live specimens, but they remained in the van. Zara scribbled and sketched in her leather-covered journal for several moments before she bolted into the cord grass alone. Aaron knew he wouldn't see her for a long time.

With his mind sluggish from the humidity, he scuffed through stinging brush and pine until the sun was shoulder high. He disturbed crows, wading birds, and one slender water snake he failed to lay a hand on. Stevie worked within sight for a while, taking plenty of breaks to sigh and slap at insects. Then Aaron was absolutely alone, making his way toward higher ground, rooting and prying and lifting, hoping he'd be the lucky one and praying he'd know how to play his luck.

In his solitude, the brackish pools and stunted vegetation began to take on a new look. He saw colors he couldn't quite name and became hungry in a way that had nothing to do with food. Shaw would have hated it, slopping around in the mud, breaking his back for something unconnected to horizon and sky, but Aaron was somehow thrilled by the difference. Zara was right. It was possible to feel your way across the land. When he sighted a cottonmouth sunning itself on a whitened log, he stared at it until it gaped its pearly jaws in protest.

Once, Zara appeared to him across the bitter-scented elbow of a creek. She beckoned with urgency. When he arrived at her side, she pointed to the deflated carcass of a long-legged bird, its eye sockets picked clean by the fiddler crabs that scuttled out of sight when he reached for the opalescent point of its bill. "An avocet," he said, "they're kind of pretty when they're alive."

"Do you have a family?" The question came from nowhere.

He wiped his hand on his shirt and thought of what was left and what he could count on. "My mom works in town."

"Yeah, well, my parents are both biology professors, and I still love this crap. Can you believe that? Out here in this heat? You'd think I'd have my own territory." She turned in a tight circle on her heels, looking up as if her search included the air.

"You do okay. You know a lot."

"True," she said with a brisk smile. "I work hard. Do you have a girlfriend? I probably ought to know that."

"No." He thought of Gina Owens. Salty tequila kisses, damp hands chafing a damp bathing suit. "Not like you mean."

"God, I thought you'd all be paired up out here, get married when you're sixteen."

"It happens some. I'm saving money for a boat."

"Don't need girls? All right. I mean I sort of have a boyfriend back home, an older guy, but he doesn't care so much. You're cute. And good about birds." She waved toward the torn avocet. "Thanks for your help on that." Then she was gone.

Lunch was a sullen time. Everyone was empty-handed except David, who had scraped a large black snake off the pavement of Highway 12. Its body was smashed flat, but he seemed pleased with the discovery, as though leathery roadkill was exactly what his attention deserved. He measured the snake's skull and jaws several times. Finally Aaron interrupted, saying he needed to leave for work. David set down his calipers and swept a hand across Aaron's shoulder, barely touching him. He thanked him for coming.

"You'll be back, right?" Zara glanced up from her journal. She hadn't even looked at him since they'd returned. "We haven't really talked yet. And you know things. We're definitely stuck."

"Unless Jed has bagged our guy," Stevie said. "I'll bet he has."

"No way." That was what she said, but she only mouthed the words, and Aaron was the only one who saw her.

"We can put our heads together if you want," David said, slipping back into his role as mentor, compact and steady. "Plan a trip for later this summer."

"Then Aaron should come to dinner and eat our icky food and give me some ideas about this damn snake." Her fingers furled among the thick, creamy pages of her journal. He liked how he couldn't predict her, how she seemed planted everywhere at once. He kept hearing David's words about smart people making use of small chances, the increments.

"I could bring some crabs to eat . . . if you like them and all. I can get plenty." He tried not to sound anxious.

"Why not? I dare you." Zara revealed a row of neat, square teeth. "Come out and feed the starving."

"I'll do it," he replied, and he didn't even look to David for confirmation, couldn't bear to, but turned to make his way down the spur of Old Hammock Road, then to camp and his bike. Zara had challenged him outright, finally speaking a jagged language he recognized—boy-girl talk, bullshit, sass. He reconsidered her body, a slender bone kit that barely made him thrum, and thought how that might be managed. She wasn't like Gina Owens who begged him to go skinny-dipping with her, made him suffer that, and returned little more than a baby doll's laugh. The thing about Zara was she didn't know how to limit her ambitions. And he somehow wanted to grab onto that trait, that stubbornness, and not let it go.

After his shift with Vernon, he rode to Shorty's, planning to run the skiff north where he had a string of pots he hadn't checked in two days. A dozen soft-shells? Two? He wondered how many crabs would be enough and how he'd ever have time to sort them, get them cooked, before the sun went down. Then the skiff's starter gave him trouble like it always did when he was in a hurry. He swore to himself, thinking Zara would get exactly what she wanted—a chance to mock him—assuming he had the guts to go to the campground empty-handed. He considered calling Flora at the warehouse and asking her to sell him someone else's catch on credit. Then he had a trickier idea. Shorty dropped lines in this cove and the next one over; Aaron could see orange-bellied markers floating less than a quarter mile away. He'd occasionally tended business for his friend and knew how to work those coves, but he'd never done it without permission. The rules about messing with another guy's territory were almost biblical. Still, the crabs were for a girl, and Shorty always advised extreme measures when it came to girls. Hoping for luck, he throttled away from the dock and tried not to look over his shoulder.

He had tied up and was unloading his buckets when Shorty banged out of his house with a little girl toddling behind him.

"Did it go good?" His friend stopped short of the dock, hands gripping his belt buckle. "I hope it did cause I been stuck in the damn house babysitting—my sister kills me if I leave Kayleen for one second—but it looked for a while from the window like you were stealing my crabs."

He knew Shorty was kidding. "I got a few peelers—fifteen, I think. Left the rest out there if that's okay."

"Nothing's okay, man. Why were you into my pots? I checked them this morning."

He jiggled the sharp wire handles of his buckets. "I didn't have time to run mine. I'm gonna pay you, make a good deal like we always do. I just need to feed some people tonight."

"Who? Those campground geeks?" Shorty grabbed his niece by the elbow and jerked her off the plank walkway to the dock. "You must be losing it, man. Lucas heard you went back to see that schoolteacher. They paying you? Is there something up there with tits?"

"I. . . ."

"God damn right." Shorty was louder and raspier now. "And she's nothing. I've seen her. I checked it out. And all I know worth knowing is that you're turning into your dead uncle Shaw O'Neal, breaking the law around here like you don't need it. You don't fuck with my stuff unless I ask you to. No man does. Ever."

He could hardly believe how Shorty's words dried and shrank him. "I'm good for the money."

"Damn right, you are. And I'll charge plenty." Shorty swung Kayleen onto his hip like she was a coil of wet line. "I'm just glad I was here to see the show. Can't wait to run down to the store and tell everybody what an asshole thief you are."

"Come on. Jesus." He was finally able to feel as mad as he needed to be. "You don't have to get all pissed. It's not like I'm lying."

Shorty twisted around on his way to the house. "It is to me. I caught you. And you know what that's like around here, don't you? Try and recall."

Later, when the crabs had been deep-fried and were draining on paper towels, when the queasiness of swallowing a dozen perfect explanations began to pass, he remembered the motto they'd all had when they were younger and trying to find trouble and dodge it at the same time. Lie low. It was advice for cards and girls, maybe more. Shaw had been careful to live that way, well inside himself. He made his decisions alone. And Shaw had been easy to admire because he appeared to know so many secrets—about fishing and hunting, about people and the ignorant messes they found themselves in. Aaron wondered now if that trait had really given Shaw any extra power. His uncle had risked everything—including his reputation—to get money for the doctors and keep the bank from repossessing the *Katie B.* He shouldn't have braved the weather that day. Bankruptcy couldn't have been so bad. Aaron had learned failure was survivable—he was still learning it—yet Shaw hadn't even considered the possibility, God damn him, hadn't even tried to adapt. He heard Shorty's recriminations again in his head. Liar. Thief. His face burned into a sweat. He could take the skiff out into the Sound, way out, and drift into the night, forget the new people, forget his friends, respect nothing but the tidal currents that had no loyalties. But he wouldn't. He'd to go back to the campground because he'd said he would and because it would cost him so much to do so.

He looked foolish bouncing into camp with buckets swinging from his handlebars, and the guys let him hear about it. He recoiled just as he should have, jerky and clownish, but it wasn't enough. They were cranky and restless even though they'd somehow gotten hold of a twelve-pack of cheap beer. No one was interested in cutting him slack. Finn and Stevie both made a point of saying they didn't like crabs.

He looked around for Zara. When he didn't see her, he concentrated on arranging the meal, understanding that the guys wanted him to keep to himself.

Jed approached him from behind while he rummaged in a cooler for cocktail sauce, maybe some mayonnaise. "Your girlfriend is on the beach with David, swimming or whispering in Latin, or whatever the hell it is they do. We thought you'd want to know."

He squashed the impulse to take Jed on nose to nose, even though it's what his grandpa would have done. He glanced over his shoulder instead, smiling into Jed's bloodshot eyes. "We got some time then. How about we all take a swim?"

"I don't swim," Jed replied.

"He's not going while *they're* on the beach," giggled Finn.

Aaron looked down at his hands, which were wrist deep in ice. He wished his whole body would go numb so he didn't have to feel embarrassment singe his skin. Then he heard Jed curse and turned to see David coming across the dunes with Zara in tow. David was wearing cut-off jeans and flip-flops, his body a slab of white belly and thick hair. Zara looked oddly piecemeal in a gaudy floral bathing suit. They steadied one another down the steep slope of sand, and the sight of David's arm against Zara's hip clubbed at Aaron's empty stomach.

"Oh my God, dinner. I'm so glad you're here." Zara practically sang her words, whipping her beach towel above their heads, but he could hear the slippage in her voice. She hadn't been prepared for him.

He stood, hoping to make himself lean and solid. "You can eat the crabs like sandwiches, they're good that way. I brought some bread." He looked at Zara as coolly as he could, trying not to take in the hard, wet points of her breasts.

"I'm getting dressed first," she announced.

"Sure. Go ahead." He turned to see David crawling into his tent, a towel draped over his head like a soggy veil.

They all ate greedily, not even pretending they had better manners. Stevie broke off his diet of corn chips and cola to taste a crab, which he finally devoured in a slather of white meat and crumbs. Dr. Oskar emerged from his tent just long enough to make a sandwich. He was busy meditating, Jed said, trying to make sense of what the island and its eccentric ecosystems were telling him.

It wasn't long before they began to talk about the snake. "We're big screwups," Jed said, lying flat on his back with a groan. "I can't believe David got us so far off track."

"It's not his fault," Zara said. "This isn't supposed to be easy. Remember how long it took Fountain and Black to find—"

"You still believe he's God, go ahead. You're not objective anyway. I'm just saying the snake's a goner. Extinct. Dr. O. practically admitted as much."

"I vote we try the mainland next, if we gotta vote." Finn had removed his glasses; the nakedness of his face made him look almost calm. "We might find something near Alligator River."

"That's not the same, not *sticticeps*," Zara snapped.

"So give it up, Zara. Or cry to David about it on your own time."

"Jed's right," Aaron whispered, or he thought he'd whispered, but the bickering stopped and he could see them all looking at him. "The island's changed, changing too fast my grandpa used to say. The geese don't come down like they did, or some of the ducks. Your snake—the king snake or whatever—could be gone too."

"You'd swear to that?" Zara glared at him, and he realized how much he wanted to be on the side against her.

"No, don't swear to anything. Island's too unpredictable for that. I'm just saying nobody I know has ever seen your kind of snake."

"Now this is what we need," Jed said. "Real local wisdom. I wish you'd spoken up before. This sure beats the tourist shit that gets peddled down here. Pirates. Mustang ponies."

Aaron shrugged. "We had pirates."

"Yeah, okay. But half that stuff is made up, it's got to be. Just good stories."

He paused to wipe his greasy hands. It was something new to be in the middle like this, powerful and slippery and at risk. "I don't know, the Howards claim kin to Blackbeard's crew. They're pretty fierce about it."

"What about you and your mom?" Zara said, and he could hear her baiting him. "What's your claim to fame?"

"Nothing. Fishermen and hunters on both sides for more than a hundred years. And lots who joined the Coast Guard."

"No pirates?" Finn laughed. "I'm damn disappointed."

"My uncle knew some guys who ran marijuana through the inlet a few times. It wasn't worth the trouble, I guess. Shaw didn't like to talk about it. Nobody does."

"Smugglers, huh? That's pretty good." Jed sat up and rubbed at his mouth. "You must get a lot of that down here, guys cutting corners. There's nobody who cares enough to stop you."

Jed was teasing him, he knew that, but that wasn't the worst of it. He should have said what he believed to be true, that it took courage and conviction and luck to make it as an honest man out here. That an independent life was so impossible. Instead, he'd mentioned the thing that was forbidden in his family, and in his own head as well, and he'd encrusted the words in a tingling, boyish boast.

Suddenly Zara was standing in front of him. He could see the oval bruises on her shins. "I'm sitting down," she said quietly. "I'd like to hear whatever you have to say about your life."

He realized, too late, that he'd hemmed himself in. They expected something from him now. He swirled his warm beer, pausing, but all he could clarify in his mind was how he wanted to tell Zara, just Zara, a good story about the island. Something that proved how wild and original his home could be.

"There was a storm when I was little," he bluffed, "like about five years old, so I don't remember too much except we lost our electricity for a few days, which happens a lot down here. It was in the fall, hurricane season, and the best time for fishing if you're one that goes to the Gulf Stream. There was talk of a gale coming in, but that's not always so predictable, and if you've got good radar and a radio, well, most people make out all right." He thought about Shaw, how he was so meticulous with his equipment and so disdainful of what it sometimes told him. "Several boats went out that morning. The tuna were running real good off Diamond Shoals and tuna's good money. The boats left. Storm swung in before they knew it."

"Don't tell me," Jed interrupted. "They found some guy floating on a piece of wood a hundred days later."

"No," Aaron said harshly. "That hardly ever happens. Most boats go down, they take the captain with them."

"So what's the deal?"

"Nothing much at first," he continued. "All the boats rode it out except for one. New boat, top of the line. She didn't come back."

"What was her name?" Zara seemed to have closed her eyes.

"I don't remember . . . I can't," he stuttered. "Doesn't matter. She never made it."

"Okay, so what next?" Finn pointed at him. "Ghosts or what? Some dead guy come stand at the end of your bed with seaweed in his hair?"

He understood then that they wouldn't believe him. They couldn't take in Grandpa's favorite tale, the one where the nameplank of the boat floated for miles until it arrived at its home dock, the splintered name of the lost vessel knocking against the pilings until the captain's family found it and shivered. That was a story for islanders, so queer and spirit-filled it had to be trusted. He'd heard it all his life. But mainlanders didn't think like that. They loved the dull fences of logic, and they'd never ridden a storm large enough to swallow a life besides. The unspoken story, the simple one that haunted him, would only bore them. He couldn't tell them about Shaw. What did they know about delinquent boat payments and huge bills from a cancer doctor? What did they care about the turn of mind it took to lead a silent, overworked man to anchor offshore in cruel weather, waiting, waiting for the illegal cargo that might buy him a few more months on the water? What had they ever heard of debt and family? Grandpa thought it was fitting they'd never found one shred of the *Katie B.*; he told his grandson that. There was nothing left to eulogize but rumor. *A man lost at sea is a man lost,* the old man said, and the parched clarity of that statement sucked him toward his own death.

"Go on," Zara whispered.

"No." He blinked at the childish burn behind his eyes. "You don't want to hear it."

"Why? Did your dad die like that? Is that why it's just you and your mom?"

"My dad is a jerk who lives in Philadelphia."

"Oh." She covered her mouth theatrically, but no one laughed. The guys looked down into their laps like they hoped he would disappear. Which he tried to do. Zara caught up with him just after he'd grappled his way onto his bike.

"I want us to get along," she said. "Maybe take a walk on the beach later. Talk."

"You've got David and everybody else. You'll get plenty of attention." He hung his head as he spoke, swallowing the wet effort of each word.

"Well, David *is* my teacher," she said. "I thought you were smart enough to know how that works. It shouldn't bother you."

She dropped a hand onto his forearm then, and he watched her do it. It was like watching a strange, intrepid moth land on glass. "Doesn't matter if I'm bothered or not. I got nothing to do here. I'm going home."

Her fingers stiffened. Then she stepped aside, shoving both hands through her hair until the skin of her brow was shiny and tight. "All right," she said. "Sure. If you say you have to."

He pedaled past the empty gatehouse with his chin outstretched, gulping thick ocean air. He'd left his buckets behind, but what the hell, he could replace them. Next week he'd see if Flora needed extra help at the warehouse. He'd sweat until he sweat bright money, patch things up with Shorty as well as he could. He'd have no debts. He was thinking that when he reached the entrance to the campground, the wide unlit curves of the highway stretching north and south along the pale phalanges of the dunes. And there was David Pryor squat at the edge of the road, sifting through the sand between his feet.

"You're leaving," he said after Aaron locked his brakes into a dry, scratchy halt.

Aaron nodded.

"It's Zara, isn't it? She has that effect on people, drives them away because she's so inconsistent. She pretends things." David was dressed in a blue shirt and khakis, his hair combed. He looked too tidy to be straying by himself. "Did she tell you about her mother and how sick she is?"

"She said they worked at a college, her mom and dad. Said they're scientists."

"That's typical. Another fib, though not one you need to protect yourself against. Her mom is a doctor who's had to give up her practice because of arthritis. Very sad. Her father teaches at the high school with me."

So they'd both lied, boy and girl. Changed their surfaces for each other, or for no real reason at all.

David took a step forward, then squared himself as though he were in front of a blackboard. "Did she tell you how close we are? Because if she did, I'd have to say it's true. She's gifted and vulnerable, always needed lots of support. I've gotten a little involved."

"It's none of my business."

"You're polite to say that, but it *is* your business. We called you in."

The anger of the past hour, or maybe the months of his life before that, tightened around his jaw. "You know what? I don't much care about your problems. This has been too weird. I thought you just wanted to find your old snake, but it's not like that. You all mess with whatever you can."

"Do we? You wanted to be around us. You're curious like you damn well ought to be. And suspicious. You said your grandfather was a waterman, right? I'll bet you come by your suspicion naturally."

"What's that supposed to mean?" His hands became half-fists.

"Maybe it means you learned a lot from your grandfather, the people you grew up with. I can be pretty sentimental—I think you're lucky to be on this island. You live where life is harsh. Not simple, I'd never say that, but there's plenty humbling about the forces out here. So much is stripped down. The romance is long gone. I could study a place like this all my life, try to figure out how the fauna hangs on and adapts. It's what I need to do—search for that crafty king snake, then search for something else. The cluttered world I'm from back home—I'm not so good at figuring that out. Terrible, in fact."

"So you mess around with Zara?"

"Not the way you're thinking, but in other ways maybe. I'm weak. I like admiration. I told myself this team thing would work for all of us—*sticticeps* too—but we keep getting in the way of our own discoveries." He smiled to himself, his eyes deep, dark blanks. "We'll try again soon. It's exhilarating."

That ended it. They could hear the surf pounding

and shushing behind them, making their tattered conversation complete. Aaron left as David Pryor resumed his crouch, his eager fingers prospecting for what couldn't be seen. He cycled home with the wind at his back.

Vernon didn't give him the note until late afternoon, after Aaron had paid for sandwiches for both of them out of his own pocket. The note was from Zara. It said they'd left that morning but would be back in August, at least she and David would be. She asked him to keep looking for *L.g. sticticeps,* for her sake, and as a friend. She included a Wilmington phone number and address below a bold initialed Z. He crumpled the note in his hand, then smoothed it flat again when he realized it was written on a page torn from her journal. On the back were several light pencil sketches of the king snake as it ought to appear. Slung-jawed, thick-browed, hungry.

That evening he snuck over to Shorty's and picked up the skiff. It was filled with rotten chum and busted oyster shells, maybe some piss, which he cleaned up as well as he could, hoping Shorty would feel like the sabotage made them even. Then he headed for his own pots. The routine would be a relief. The sloshing, kiltering weight of the traps, the slimy thickness of the lines—those were the kinds of back-wrenching challenges he could meet. He ran the boat into the sun until he was clear of the eelgrass that bedraggled the tide. He saw Shorty's new neighbor, Mr. Hewitt, fly-fishing on the flats but didn't wave to him. They guy was an artist, too green and breathless to be trusted. He passed Eli Howard's where dogs roiled in the backyard, then the Stevens's backwater where Cort Stevens's shad boat was dry-docked beneath a crude lean-to, a faded relic of a fading time.

The skiff's punky engine quit on him near the Austins' quarter of the marsh. It didn't so much stop as sputter until he cut the ignition in disgust. Spark plugs—he'd have to dig through Shaw's damnable cans to find replacements. He drew the oars from beneath the sticky, chum-stained thwarts and began to row, hoping for some lift from the tide. Then it struck him. This was where Zara's snake would be, near the spartina picket of the marsh, exactly where David assumed it wouldn't live. He looked toward the scraggle of wax myrtle and live oak that hung above the shore. Surely there was a niche there, away from the water moccasins and ordinary king snakes, amid tidal wrack and ruin, right along the stinking backside of everyone's beach paradise. The idea filled him, hot and rude, until he burst into laughter that echoed onshore. He liked the thought of *sticticeps* inhabiting the same neglected crevices of the island he did, living the same relentless life. He'd hack his way along the shore near Mrs. Austin's and find the damn thing one day, and he'd never say a word about it. Simply seeing that snake, thick and armored and deliberate in its patterns, would answer any questions he might have. There'd be nothing to do but leave it alone.

He dipped the oars into the jade trail of current and

pulled for Grandpa's spindly dock. His head said he'd be living there, in the reopened house, come winter. His blood told him he had endless labors before him if he wanted to remake the life of an island man. Endless labor, endless repair.

North of Fear, South of Kill Devil

I couldn't have chosen a worse day.

The air is plank heavy with a hint of wind on its edge. Sky and sea are joined at the horizon like a nickel hinge, and I know we'll have a storm before noon. I'm supposed to join the fleet today, but if I go by the bait shop, Teeter may tell me Captain Finch won't be sailing. Teeter is skeptical about my plans. He thinks I should stick to surf fishing. *Come on, Miz Tally,* he'll say, *they're pullin' in a few blue at the Point. And you know the croakers is always good.*

Still, I want to end something by motoring through the inlet with Finch and the Edwards boys. Something strangling and rangy. Captain Bead Finch will let me on board the trawler *Fiona* as long as he believes I'm working for a Yankee newspaper. Once he finds out what I'm really after, how I've fooled him, he'll toss me ashore. Teeter wants to protect me from the ridicule that's thick as caulk down here on Cape Hatteras. He doesn't want to see me laughed off the docks. But Teeter doesn't know how useful humiliation can be. They'll never forget me if I duck out of the cabin in new boots, heavy gloves, no camera or notepad in my hands. They'll gawk when I volunteer to sluice the hold. They'll gauge me as the foolish outside gal who tried to make a stir. The rest of me, whatever it might've been, will be forever filleted away.

Take my attempt to con myself onto a Coast Guard cutter, for example. My impersonation of an oceanographer dazzled the first lieutenant I spoke to, and his goodwill almost saw me silhouetted against the rigging of the *Pamlico.* But name-dropping wasn't enough. They found me out. The lieutenant was very sympathetic, however, when I told him that the death of my husband, Submarine Commander Benjamin Ford (Ben was an historian, a submariner of sorts), had driven me to extremes. Commander Ford, I told him, always wished he'd joined the Guard. Wanted to end his days topside, I said, saluting the shallows at Cape Fear from the stately bow of a craft like the *Pamlico.*

I was escorted to the gates of the Portsmouth compound by a red-haired ensign. There were brown pelicans on the roof of the gatehouse, angular and silent, resting amid the fray.

That day was a turning point. Ben had been dead five months, and I finally began to see something beyond the milky carapace that surrounded me. I hadn't made it onto the ship, but for the first time in weeks I had hands that could do more than donate Ben's books to the college, hands that could mold more than the shivering bowl of his skull. After months of habitual response, I felt like talking. To myself. To Teeter. To anyone. I wanted to be a citizen.

Then I saw her—the bilge-stained *Fiona,* bow as blunt as a heel—and I felt the long, dark pitch of the waves once again.

I cross the road and trot into the bait shop, looking like I need a new shark rig or four dozen steel leaders, something serious.

Teeter knows better. He's been at the counter since five-thirty, busily assuring the tourists they've got two or three hours before a storm hits. He's sold a lot of bait, telling me when I come through the door he's got only one container of bloodworms left, I'd better get on the stick.

"Fish the Sound side today, Miz Tally," he says, bending over a carton of Marlboros. "The flounder's good anywhere till the tide goes out."

"Will Finch leave?" I examine the rack of sunglasses.

"No, ma'am. Forecast is real bad."

"Tomorrow?"

"Not likely."

Teeter is easier on me than he is on most newcomers, partly because I told him right off that I wanted to winter here. I didn't care about summer, wasn't interested in the fall bluefish run. Teeter makes money on the side drumming up business for the charter boats, but once he decides you're not a customer, he does one of two things: ignores you or makes you his own. He ignored me at first because he thought I was part of the long stream of artists that flows onto the Outer Banks of North Carolina with the warm weather.

"I seen the way you dressed," he told me. "Shorts and sandals. I was sure you was painting them mangledy dunes to sell for Christmas."

I told him I was just a forty-six-year-old widow. Nothing more.

"Husband a waterman?"

He meant well, wondering whether Ben had been in the navy or merchant marine. They respect that down here—nostalgia for the way men used to sail and the sights they used to see. What was once a refuge for pirates has become a haven of regret, home to those who still hope to go down with the ship.

"No," I whispered, "Ben was a teacher and a fool."

Teeter pretends it's a thing I never said.

I take a small, glassy-eyed mullet out of the cooler, and while Teeter is ringing me up, he starts to laugh and tells me it's too late, Bill Fender has already been in looking for me. If I insist on fishing the surf, I'll get caught.

"Shoulda bought bloodworms," he says. "Played it safe."

I tell him I'm not running from Bill Fender.

"Just warning you," he says.

"Thanks," I say, leaving him my change. "You take care of yourself. Buy a necklace or something."

"Yep," he says, fingering the three or four gold chains tangled around his throat. "Gotta keep up with the surfer boys."

Sure enough, Bill Fender is sitting on the weathered steps of my cottage. He's wearing Bermudas, walking shoes, a Princeton T-shirt, and a stained sun visor. He doesn't have any fishing gear with him because Bill isn't on Hatteras Island for recreation. Bill is here to finish his novel.

He met me at the bait shop a month ago, and since I didn't look anxious enough to be a tourist, he decided I was a native, or a longtime resident at least. Wearing a madras shirt and a mask of zinc oxide, he introduced himself and said he was aboard to do a little writing. He said I looked knowledgeable and friendly, perhaps I could give him some advice on getting to know the area. I told him there were information bureaus in every village.

"No," he said. "I want to live here, not wander. You must know what I mean."

I wasn't a writer, I said. I had other business.

Teeter was listening in, of course, and he sniffed a big one in Mr. Bill Fender.

"Farley Midgett runs a good tour of the Banks out of the marina," he said, leaning on the counter like he does. "Sound side, surf side—one day in his boat'll show you what you want."

"No, thank you," Fender said. "I'm after a particular angle."

Well, Teeter was still sure he could hook him, and he

rang up Bill's plastic shovels and potato chips and Coca-Colas in grand, slow style, talking the whole time. Relieved, I went next door to the post office. Bill Fender stopped me on the way out.

"I'll be reasonable," he said. "The fellow in there says you're a good guide. I'll pay the going rate."

I almost told him he was being taken for a ride, but it occurred to me that Bill Fender might be the distraction I needed. I could take him on as a client and show him what I didn't know. After a day, maybe two days, he'd realize he was in the hands of a midlander, a woman who didn't understand the mysteries of any coast, much less this one. He'd feel cheated. And I would be released.

We shook hands.

"Got your family here?" I tried to sound salty and skeptical.

"My wife and two children are at the cottage, but they won't be a bother. Terri understands what this means to me." He peered into his grocery bags as if they, too, were filled with the right kind of atmosphere. "We'll have all the time we need."

Unfortunately, Bill Fender was easier to please than either Teeter or I imagined. I took him to useless locales at inappropriate times, and he remained curious and full of questions. After three days, I'd had enough. I told Bill I'd been "aboard" only a few months; that there were not, in fact, any shipwrecks off the pier at Avon. To my surprise, he didn't express shock but something he called mature gratitude. He thanked me.

So he still comes looking for me when he wants to reset his particular angle, that local perspective he believes will make him a truer soul.

"Morning, Bill."

"Good morning, Thalia. Sorry I missed you at the shop." He tugs at his visor. "Didn't want to disturb you here."

"What can I do for you?" I unlock the small ground-level room that holds my bucket and tackle.

"I see you're fishing."

"Hope to. Storm will hit soon."

"Yes, well, I was wondering . . . I'd like to get out."

"You're out," I wave my hand toward the ocean, "about as far as you can go."

"No, I need to get away. Not from Terri and the kids," he adds, though that seems to be the truth of the matter. "From the book. It's swallowing me, Thalia, and I know you'll be a help."

"Bill, I don't think I know much that'll help you. I fish. I'm your neighbor. I was married to a man who could have bronzed your ears with the history of the Great Lakes. That's about it."

"But you're a smart woman." His voice peals with the high-pitched conviction of a boy.

"I think I've already been swallowed," I mutter, wiping my tiny scimitar of a knife on my pants.

"We could just take a walk."

I think about how little that will cost me, then reach for my pole. Bill Fender is not the worst companion in the world. "All right. We can go up to the Refuge if the storm doesn't last. Do a little bird-watching. See what's settled in after the rain." He agrees, Ivy League grace restored with a nod of his head. He wishes me luck. I tell him I'll pick him up at two if the sky is clear.

I head to the beach, struggling as I weave past the sand myrtle and blanket flower. It's a walk that hasn't gotten easier, even after several months. The sand is deep, and the fifty yards from my house to the crest of the dunes is a landscape without much reward. It is skittered by lizard and ghost crab, plundered by crow and gull. The mammals who live here—mice and rabbit and fox—are wary and thin.

Hatteras Island is a sandbar. A big hurricane would bury it, and I sometimes imagine what it would look like then, swept clean of house trailers and garbage cans and billboards. No more sandwich wrappers, no more Jeep Cherokees or neon sails. The bait shop would collapse into the silty ripple of a tidal flat, and only the Buxton lighthouse would remain, water lapping at its waist, its beacon sweeping over a land lost to depth and reflection.

It's a vision I enjoy.

There are few people on the beach. One or two fishermen near the pier, a pair of ambling beachcombers to the north. The sun is a shapeless glare, still thickly blanketed by clouds. I rig my pole quickly, slitting the mullet into strips like the expert I pretend to be. My line, held steady by a four-ounce weight, is in the water before five minutes have elapsed.

My first few casts are fruitless. The surf is not particularly high since the tide's backing out, but the water is rough, churning green and brown above the undertow. I finally bring in about what I expect—a misfit bluefish and a shark, a twenty-inch dogfish I throw back after I work the hook free of its snapping jaws. By then the wind is chopping into the water enough to convince me to call it a day.

As I'm stowing my gear, the sky grows dark, and I recall Ben's theory of light. Ben lived all over the country—San Francisco, Boston, Memphis—before he settled outside Chicago. He was convinced people are affected by their relationship to the sun. Easterners watch the sun rise over the water, he whispered; it drives them into their day. But the West Coast, there the sun flares and falls over an infinity of ocean. There, sunset befits comfort and peace.

Ben was madly speculative in short bursts, and I loved him for it. But I can't help asking what I always asked when he was alive. What about islanders, I would say. What about water all around? Since we were best when we were sparring, he didn't respond to my question with any seriousness. And I'm not sure what he'd say now, since he would never, ever have confined himself to this strip of shell-strung sand and vegetation. Not even to grieve.

But as I stand beneath the first peals of thunder, alone

as only the whipping fabric of the wind can make me, I imagine him telling me to stop my struggle, to keep my eyes open and peering. There is light and current all around, he says. Find it, sight it, watch it fall away.

It rains hard for several hours, water blowing through the porch window I keep open. The cottage, which I've rented for twelve months, sways on its stilts in a way I've come to love. It leans and rights itself without creaking or jerking, its balance as finely tuned as the balance of a surfer. It is a ride I like to fall asleep to.

I head to the Bronco when I spot a crescent of clear sky, before the rain actually stops. If Bill Fender isn't ready, not able to get away from sturdy Terri and the kids, so much the better.

But he is dauntless. When I arrive, his family is asleep in the muffled rumble of air-conditioned rooms, and Bill is reading on his small front porch. It doesn't matter that I'm early. He enjoys the spontaneity. "One moment, Thalia," he says, saluting me with his magazine. "I'll don my gear and be right out."

Don? Gear? I look down at my worn rubber boots, my second-rate binoculars, my hat and can of bug spray. I remind myself to be patient.

Bill climbs into the Bronco with binoculars and an old military canteen. He's wearing a hunting vest with bulging pockets, and he smells sweet, like a rind rotting in the sun. As he settles into his seat, I realize he's splashed himself with some sort of aftershave, the kind you might expect to smell on the cooler breezes of the Vineyard or Long Island Sound.

We speed north on Highway 12, passing a rusty Winnebago and a trio of long-distance cyclists on the outskirts of town. In twenty minutes we're at the southern edge of the Pea Island Wildlife Refuge. I drive to a public ramp and park the Bronco on oily, tire-packed sand.

"Let's sneak out to that point." I gesture toward a long finger of grass and reeds. "I've always had luck there."

Bill is quiet. While he covers his freckled arms with insect repellent, he nods rhythmically as though he's not really listening. He's preparing himself for inspiration, I guess, leaving me to provide the noise and spectacle of our outing. If I succeed, he will be reinvigorated. He can return to Terri and see in her the vital grace of an egret or the dangerous patience of a hovering hawk. Me? I suppose I'll go my own way, whirling from point to cape to cove with my stubborn unhappiness as a broad and flashing beacon.

For an hour we see nothing but gulls and the occasional unsettled duck. Then a small heron lands some fifty yards to our right. Bill Fender presses the binoculars to his eyes and fumbles for his Audubon guide. "Don't bother," I say, "it's a yellow-crowned night heron. Enjoy it."

The bird possesses a beautiful frozen poise. Its filigreed crest is delicate and light, and I remember how the sight of a bird would excite Ben. A robin building its nest, the shrill cry of a nighthawk at dusk—any creature in flight would quicken his eye. He made startling, soaring adventure out of the evident, and I sometimes hated him for it.

Bill Fender watches the heron for a while, then lowers his glasses and settles back into the space we've made for ourselves. He's covered in sweat. The binoculars have left pink half-circles under his eyes.

"This is good for me, Thalia," he whispers.

I smile.

"I could never do this with Terri, you know. She doesn't understand Nature."

I lift my eyebrows.

"I need this . . . this interaction . . . to remind myself of the essence of things. That's what the book's about, of course," he hisses. "Essences. Male and female. The immutable truth."

Alerted by the muttering, the heron takes flight. Then it's just me and Bill—the essence of human dissatisfaction. And the last thing I want to witness is a confession, the dribble of personal failure followed by a leak of hope. Bill Fender is a writer, for God's sake. Can't he do better? Doesn't he have any imagination?

"I've known a number of women, Thalia," he continues. "None have been like you."

I'm on my feet in a split second, binoculars beating at my hip. "You're way off track, Bill. I came here for the waterfowl, nothing else."

I walk quickly when I'm mad. Bill Fender follows as

well as he can. Until today, our talk has always been harmless—the structure of his dreams, his kids' IQs—nothing that really mattered. Now he starts in on Man and Woman. Inscrutable, immutable. I don't want to hear it, I really don't. I've earned my ruined heart. I can't believe Bill Fender doesn't respect that.

I stop short of the road and let him catch up. His skin is flushed, eyes weak and watery. When he sees I'm waiting, he squares his shoulders and resets his visor. His feet are covered with slick brown ooze.

"Thalia, I don't know what I—"

"You were out of line, Bill. William. This was supposed to be bird-watching. I took you at your word."

"I didn't mean anything, I just—" A regretful smile pulls at his lips. "I wanted to discuss the book."

"That book isn't real," I say, heading to the Bronco. "It's fiction, it doesn't concern me." The Bronco has been baking in the sun, but I get in anyway. Bill Fender stands frozen on the sticky pavement, his eyes sweeping back and forth like the arm of a metronome. For a long time neither of us moves.

The sun is hunkering down over Pamlico Sound before I'm able to put a finger on my feelings. I'm on the roof deck of my cottage, high enough to see the thick, fractured surface of the ocean. Another storm is mounting the horizon, where distant lightning flickers like hand shadows against the sky, and I'm sipping a cloudy glass of water, trying not to imagine what this evening would be like if I were still in Illinois. Ben would be planning a trip, no doubt. To Beaver Island or some park way up in Ontario. He'd be making lists in his head, not telling me a thing, creating the chaos he loved. We never left home without forgetting something—a piece of equipment, a map—that I considered crucial. But Ben, oh Ben, he was the peddler of making do, getting along, etching good times on the air.

I couldn't stand it. Haphazard exploration and random encampment. We'd spend weeks volunteering for preservation groups, moving from forests to lakes so quickly we didn't even have time to relish the poignancy of our efforts, the one beauty I thought we should savor. Ben was erratic, but strangely enough, he was a very fine historian. I don't bind *myself* to facts, he said. I'm not an event, I'm a passage of time.

He was right about that.

As I'm thinking of Ben, I realize my anger at Bill Fender is misguided. Ben is the one I'm furious with, the one who really hurt me. Bill Fender has only scraped a nerve. He's called up the feelings that overtook me when I released Ben's ashes into the breeze along Lake Michigan. When my hands finally shook themselves free of that urn, I was afire with rage. I couldn't believe he'd left me. He'd done the planning, the orchestrating. He'd woven the whole damn tapestry since the day we got married. It wasn't that I was helpless. I had money, my atrophied teaching skills. Instead, Ben left me without the one gift I'd finally learned to take from him, the thing I desperately needed. He'd left me without the imagination.

The anger remains. It keeps me from wringing myself dry with tears the way I did when I emptied our house, packing everything that ever pleased or irritated me in boxes. If only he hadn't been so stubborn. If only he'd been self-serving enough to go to a doctor. Instead, he loped on ahead, ignoring the rich, dark freckle on his chest and the frenzy of its changes until nothing could be done for him. He was sorry he hadn't tended to himself when he realized his illness had consolidated my fears. My husband would kill himself with offhand neglect; he would accept his fate with an eye to the wondrous, tumbling passage of time. And he would leave me behind, as wounded as a trout on a stringer—hooked, disoriented, flailing.

Ben always hoped I would put up with his quirks because they were generally harmless. He thought we made a good team. But if I wanted to stay home from a trip, that was fine too. He went ahead on his own, the Subaru packed to the roof with tools, canvas, dried fruit, books.

My excesses, however, weren't so benign. John Rhoden, one of Ben's colleagues, saw a great deal of me when Ben drove to Minnesota to sample a handful of the 10,000 lakes. And young Stephen—I dove into him like the neglected, aching woman I thought I was. We didn't leave the house for three days. I rearranged furniture and kitchenware. Stephen fingered most of Ben's files. And

I left it all for Ben to see. He took it in: the wine-stained counters, the tangled sheets, my pallor. I read an admonition, a pale hardness in his lips, but he didn't speak. There it is, I said. No more separation. I need to stay right with you—if you'll let me. There's not much for me to learn here on my own.

I was right, for once. We lived, traveled, and forgave together until he died during a code in the intensive-care unit. He warned me, the bastard. We tried to say our good-byes. But I kept holding on and on.

I decide to call Bill Fender. It's about nine o'clock. He'll be settling behind the heirloom desk he brought down from New York. I dial his number, thinking that for the first time in five months I'm doing exactly what Ben would advise me to do.

Bill answers.

"William. Tally Ford here. I'd like to make it up to you."

"Tally? Oh, Thalia," he says. "Hello."

"I wasn't fair to you out there."

"No, no," I hear him rolling his chair on nervous wheels, "the lady was provoked."

"Well, the lady wants to make amends. I'd like to go flounder gigging."

Bill Fender is caught off guard. I guess he expected a restrained apology, one that would make us both itch with embarrassment. "Now?" he asks.

"At the bait shop. I need to get a lantern. Just wear the right shoes," I say. "And don't hold out on me."

Gigging has been on Bill Fender's activity list for a while, but I've refused to take him since I don't like to go wading with just anybody, especially in the black of night. It will be worth the trouble this time. I'll share some of what I really know about the island and help Bill Fender fill a bucket with flounder besides. I feel good. Better than I would on Bead Finch's floating fish pail, I'm sure.

———

The bait shop is open until eleven, and Charlotte and her swarthy brother Jimbo can usually be found behind the counter for the last shift. I'm surprised to see Teeter pouring coffee for some fishermen when I come through the door. Teeter rarely works after five. Nights are his special time, he says. He roams best at night.

"Good evening, Teeter." I raise a hand. "Gentlemen."

The fishermen nod and grin. They appear to have holed up with their Jim Beam during the storm.

"Miz Tally," Teeter shouts. "Please tell me you went after blue on the Point."

"Nope, stayed home. Hauled in more shark."

"Shoulda known better."

"What are you doing here, anyway?" I ask. "Shouldn't you be scouting the tan lines up in Buxton?"

Teeter hefts his shoulders under his ice blue shirt and turns so he can wise-eye me in profile. "Just waitin' for my date. She's a waitress. College girl."

"Oh. Didn't notice you were all dressed up."

This galls Teeter even though he saw it coming. He

wraps a forefinger in his necklaces. "And what can I do for you?" he asks. "*You* got a date? Need more bait for Bill Fender?"

"Matter of fact, I need your lantern and float. I'm taking Bill gigging."

Teeter hoots. The fishermen, who have been flirting with Charlotte, shake their heads. "Be my guest, Miz Tally. All the way," he hollers. "I'll lend you the lantern, bucket, gigs. Everything you need." He works his way past the racks of crackers and sunscreen, half-dancing with laughter. "Come on back."

In the storage room which smells of day-old fish and ammonia, Teeter hands over his gear, including a handmade gig that's striped like a candy cane. "My boyhood special," he says. "Daddy made it just for me."

I thank him, my arms heavy with the five-volt battery and underwater lamp.

"Where you going anyway?"

"Kinnakeet Station."

"Oh, Miz Tally." Teeter starts to break up.

"What?"

"That place, we're talkin' memories. I got to be a daddy and ex-boyfriend there. All in one night." Teeter pats my straining shoulder. "You and Bill Fender under them little round yaupon trees. My, my."

"Don't get carried away," I say, pushing on the door with my hip. "Mr. Fender is married, you'll recall."

"So was I once," he says, grabbing a pack of barbecued pork rinds as he follows me down the aisle.

"We're going gigging. Salt water and nails. Spiked fish."

"Oh, ho," says Teeter. "Okay. How 'bout some pork rinds for the road? Something to keep you warm."

The evening sky is the color of a sun-bleached pail. It won't rain now, but there won't be a moon either, nothing to guide me but instinct. While I wait for Bill Fender, I remember the last time I organized a fishing trip. Ben was very weak. He'd been in the hospital twice that month but insisted we go north for the weekend, to Sleeping Bear Park. I loaded the Subaru myself, packing the trunk efficiently and with a terrible feeling of failure. I didn't think we should do anything for the last time, not consciously. Ben disagreed. "I want to show you where to spread my ashes," he said, "and I want to catch some trout. With you."

He didn't have the strength. He couldn't climb the steep dunes at the park, even with my help. I cried when he waved at the children who scrambled past us, some of them just five and six years old. His breath rasped in his throat like shaved metal in a can. We never made it to where the sand falls two hundred feet into the rocking, astonishing blue of Lake Michigan. He had to describe his special spot, a grove of broken stone and cottonwood, and I had to find it later, on my own.

We couldn't fish for trout either. Ben could hardly sit up, and even an afternoon of trolling would have been too much. Still, he insisted we go out: me with the poles, the stringer, the net; him with the bait. He insisted we see morning light on the water. We drove to the Glen Lakes, and Ben sat himself on the edge of the bridge with a slim graphite rod. It was early, and several flat-bottomed boats were out for bass in the deep channels of Big Glen. The only bites we got, however, were perch—bony, greedy, fern-striped perch. Ben's small rig was struck the second it hit water, and I spent all of my time rebaiting a hook that was too tiny for his shaking hands to hold. He didn't catch anything large enough to keep—he couldn't cast any farther than the channel markers—but he kept it up, coughing and shivering, pausing once to let a merganser lead her black-crested brood beneath the bridge.

The futility and weakness infuriated me, and I told Ben so, told him I wouldn't thread another God damn leaf worm onto his God damn dimestore hook. "This is play stuff," I shouted, startling the double-bent bass fishermen. "A kid could do this. You're making it up."

Ben looked at me. I was standing behind him with the bait cup in my hand, ready to toss it into the lake, and he looked at me with a bright finish to his eyes. Then he cast his line—the empty hook as brassy and weightless and unpredictable as a dragonfly in the clear dawn air.

The abandoned life-saving station at Little Kinakeet is visible in the Bronco's headlights, a bone gray ghost. I tell

Bill Fender this is the most haunted place I know. The wind slips along the station's sagging eaves, whistling as it cannot whistle over the gritty dunes, and though the building is faceless now, scentless even, it once sheltered the capsized and the fearless. The stoic men who lived there, scraping barnacles off dinghies and hanging their pot-bleached laundry out to dry, saved lives. They cast off in high boots and slickers. They patrolled the darkened beach in tireless shifts, peering, listening, waiting for someone to go under.

Bill doesn't seem very interested—he's oddly close-mouthed—but then he's never been here alone, late at night, when the moon is full hull to the north. If Ben had ever seen this place, he would have climbed onto the roof of the empty watchtower so he could view the entire coast. He would have *lived* here, for a moment. I wish I could do that. But Ben's acts were his own deft embroidery. Mine remain a clumsy tangle.

I park near some wasted dock pilings, a few yards beyond Teeter's grove of yaupon trees. No one else is around. There is a fresh set of tire tracks, probably the ranger's, but otherwise no fishermen, no teenagers, no idle campers from Germany or Australia.

"Water ought to be good and low," I say, checking the valve on the raft. "You want to spear or work the light?"

"Whatever you think is best." Bill looks away from me, over the flat pan of the Sound.

"I'll gig then. Let's go."

Teeter's float and lantern are good ones. The light hangs maybe three inches below the water and illuminates the bottom with a golden beam that is six or seven feet in diameter. As soon as I wade in and steady the raft, we see creatures all around us, scuttling and darting into darkness. Crab, spot, finger-length eel—the water is woven with silver-threaded fins and legs. "Just move on ahead," I tell Bill. "If you see something, let me know."

Stepping carefully, I look for flounder on the lamp-lit sand. They settle on the bottom and camouflage themselves with sand thrown up by their fins. But as currents shift above them, their outlines become hieroglyphs easily read by the unfairly literate hunter.

We're barely thirty yards offshore when I gig my first fish. I strike him low, past the pectoral—a lucky shot. Bill nets him and drops him into the bucket. The water is knee high now, and as Bill hangs the net on his belt, I notice his legs look weak and hairless in the diluted light.

"I took him too low," I say. "You want to pin them behind the gills. Hard."

"Oh, you were quick, Thalia. I didn't see a thing."

"You should try it." I extend Teeter's gig like a runner's baton.

But Bill is hesitant. He looks at the fish, pierced but alive in the cloudy water of the bucket. Is he horrified? Squeamish? I can't tell. "I guess not," he says. "I ought to. You've brought me out here. But it doesn't seem quite right."

"Right?"

"You know, correct. Precise."

"This is about as precise as fishing gets, Bill. Unless you've got the swipe of a grizzly."

"No, not this," he lifts the bucket between us. "I mean the two of us out here, congregating as we are."

His voice squeaks some, as though he can't find the right tone. The slump of his shoulders tells me he's thinking about his wife.

"We're fishing, not congregating. You might remind Terri of that." I nudge the raft with my knee and its beam begins to swing—the silent bell of a useless buoy. "As I recall, *you* were the one who wanted to do this."

"Yes. You've been so accommodating, so flexible in your way. But I can't always steel myself."

"Steel yourself against what?"

"The landscape. Distress." He clears his throat for resonance. "Love."

A point beneath my sternum begins to burn. "God damn it, Bill, I will send you to hell on this raft. Don't you dare use that word."

Chastened, he drops the bucket into the water. Our flounder begins to float free.

"No, no, listen to me, Thalia. I don't love you. I . . . I'm not saying that."

"Then what are you saying? Why are you wasting my time out here? Let fat Terri and the kids take care of you."

Bill faces me, eyes and mouth invisible. His hands move vaguely, calmly, like furled sails, and I can't stop myself from trying to bring them into focus. "That's it," he whispers. "Get mad at me. Mad. You need to do this."

As I stare into the murky glow of his body, I begin to feel seasick. I think I understand a terrible thing. Bill Fender—straw man, decoy, punching bag for my frustrations—has been propping me up, and he knows it. He doesn't love me. He's right about that. But I have been using him, reducing him, all along.

When I try to move, I fall forward, splashing up to my chest in silty water. And I want to sit there forever, an out-riddled sphinx sunk in the mud. But the taste of brine on my lips brings me Ben. Ben would have allowed for weakness in anger, all this stupidity in grief. He would have owned up to his mistakes and taken his lessons gladly. He would have charged on. I glance up at Bill Fender. It occurs to me that the two of us are an undeniable island, an incongruous mass of hope and discontent rooted in a shifting sea.

"I miss him," I say. "I can't read people anymore."

"You try too hard," he says. "You won't allow anyone to help. Some of us might help."

In a moment, Bill has me by the elbow, and we are walking. The raft trails behind us like a forgotten spotlight. Bill has a good grip—I feel a quick, sure pulse across my cold palm. He doesn't talk, however; he won't go further. We both know it's enough to share the kindness of silence. The hard curl of water against the invisible bulkhead becomes louder, and I can't help but imagine a dawn-framed scene without a caption. Ben is on that pounded bulkhead, Ben is on that bridge. He is bright-eyed and swiveling, lofting his line. When I have wept again and rested, I will look for him, ready to inscribe those fearless hooks on air.

Graveyard of the Atlantic

His wife was a poet who, in cruel and important ways, was becoming lovelier and more gifted as she aged. She was close to fifty now, her hair threaded with a tarnished silver that looked warm, unkempt, in photographs. She was also thin, as whittled down as she'd ever been, and so argumentative that her friends forgave her, thinking it must be part of some performance she was putting on for herself. He knew better. Something deep had taken hold of his Lucy, a grip that felt relentless even to him. Each morning she set off on her walk through the neighbor's fields limping with tension. He followed her progress along the sun-spackled path, watched her shrink to the size of his thumb, then disappear.

Eaten up with God. That's how she tried to describe it to him, her eyes loden green in the lamplight of her study. She was being called into a dialogue; the pressure within was as physical as a tumor. "There's a fist there," she said. "An actual groping hand." He leaned toward her and responded with soft, half-lidded eyes. She rarely wanted him to make a parade of his own words.

"We could use the grant money. I've thought about going to the mountains, someplace like Montana where the altitude alone is a prayer. But it seems important—I don't know how yet—to outsmart my beliefs. All of them. So it's the coast, I think. A cottage near the ocean wouldn't be too spartan for you, would it? You'll be able to explore."

He packed a month later for Frisco, North Carolina, a tiny sprawl south of Nags Head that had neither the glamour nor the isolation he expected. Then again, he reminded himself, this was about Lucy's expectations. She would begin a fourth book of poems down there whether she actually spoke to God or not. So he boxed the SilverStone pans she'd set on the counter though he predicted she'd have little interest in cooking or eating. He zipped up a garment bag filled with batik skirts she'd never wear. The books—St. Augustine, Jung, an untranslated memoir of a French abbess, a much-thumbed Koran lent by a friend—were only talismen and would be no more useful to Lucy than shells on a string. She didn't read much when she worked, especially when she was working well. He added a few books for himself.

They made love the night before they left, and Lucy was all angles and impatience. She moved as though she was still sure of the raw allure of her body, as though their well-worn affection did not need to be coaxed or teased. The urgent pallor of her face excited him—it was like coupling with a younger, wraithlike Lucy he'd never known—and he was pleased with his own physical greed. Afterward, as his body shrank back toward imperfection, he watched his wife fall asleep. That was how it was with them, he thought. Lucy was here, then gone, while he could always be found in his watchful place.

They'd been together fifteen years. He'd been married briefly when he was young and believed he was going to be a lawyer. When it became clear he would take over the stamping plant his father had founded in Waterbury, his wife left him for a sarcastic editor of the law review. He worked, sifted through his ordinary habits, met Lucy when he was nearly forty. Her first husband had been a poet, and their mutual misbehavior as partners produced animosity and a great deal of writing, though only Lucy's poems had been much good. The ex-husband, Mark, now taught at a small college in California, a job he landed after he finally published a book. "You're damn right I keep score," Lucy announced to admirers at a party for her third book, a volume she would later tell him, her quiet husband, was calculated and weak—a charade in falsetto. "Anger, deception, even stupidity. It's all nothing unless you turn it into work." She enjoyed implying that her ex-husband had designs but too little will, just as she enjoyed keeping the anecdotes about their smash-up marriage alive.

They didn't talk much on the long drive south, ignoring even the radio. Lucy was good-humored, calm. She wore her hair in a girlish ponytail and insisted on eating breakfast biscuits at fast-food restaurants as often as they could. "We'll move among the people," she joked, slipping on an enormous pair of wraparound sunglasses that were a gift from a student. "Think of me as Yoko Ono. Escort me like that."

The cottage was small but close to the ocean. He opened the windows and whisked away a few cobwebs, then stepped onto the windswept deck and watched two large families straggle home from the beach. He cringed when he realized they'd have neighbors who would laugh and quarrel in the heat, who'd bathe cranky children in the outside shower stalls. Lucy was used to silence. But the sight of exhausted, reddened bodies pleased him a little, as well. Company would do him good; he'd have a lot of time to himself. He remembered the last two hours of their trip, how Lucy sped down the eroded coastline as though the flat, sea-gray horizon needed to be pierced.

She chose the back bedroom for her own, squeezing a cheap end table between two sets of bunks and calling it a desk. "I'll squirrel away in here," she said, opening the blue curtains decorated with golden anchors, then shutting them again. "A child's room, stale with dreams. And with the blinds down I'll be able to hear the ocean, just hear it." She seemed to anticipate his objections to the lack of air and good light because she stepped close and hugged him. "I'm happy, Chris," she said. "I can't tell you what it means to leap in like this." He returned the embrace, pressing her against his stomach until he felt her slender bones flex. But he wasn't tender. Neither of them was.

Lucy left their bed twice in the night. In the morning he showered and ate a dry bagel for breakfast without knowing whether she was in the cottage or not. He thought of her curled like a dried wasp on the mattress of a bunk, he thought of her wandering the wilderness of her mind. Instead of settling into a deck chair with the Truman biography and some coffee, he decided to make a trip to the grocery store. He wasn't to follow Lucy down her paths, not out of concern or boredom—this was their unspoken pact.

The cashier at the store hardly looked at him. She slumped over his purchases as though she were blind to new faces, had been drained by them. There was a fishing store next door—the two businesses were connected by a doorway—and he decided to go in. It looked like a place where he could ask questions.

The floor of the Frisco Rod & Gun Shop was crowded with bristling racks of fishing poles and glass-front cases of knives, diving watches, and reels. Standing there with his grocery bags at rest on his hips gave him the same feeling he'd had when he stepped onto the floor of the stamping plant. A good feeling, warm and hard beneath his diaphragm. This was a serious, well-grounded place—a business that knew its business—and he quickly decided he'd buy some tackle or whatever for himself. It took him a moment to realize he'd walked in on a fiercely whispered argument.

A boy in a baggy blue slicker was standing near the cash register, his scabbed fist wrapped tight around a rod that was much taller than he was. The boy had close-cropped hair and a skinny, crooked face that seemed to splotch with humiliation as he listened to the muscular young man who leaned from behind the counter. The boy shook his head, dug his chin into his chest, then shook his head again. The man, who was blond and bearded and stiff with impatience, reached for the rod with an open hand. The boy jerked it away and jammed it into a bucket filled with plastic sand spikes. "You know I don't got the money," he wailed, kicking at air with his shredded sneaker. "Damn you, anyhow." And he ran from the store, coat flapping. Chris thought he could smell the boy's fury in the braided scent of rubber and stale french fries that roiled past him. He was also sure the boy had looked at him before uttering his phlegmy curse.

The blond man made no apologies. He acted as if Chris were the first customer of the day. "Set your things down. Look around. Just let me know what I can do." The man rerolled the sleeves of his plaid shirt above his elbows as he spoke, and Chris suddenly felt dizzy with responsibility. The grocery bags slipped onto his thighs, almost beyond control. "I've never been here," he said too loudly. "I'd like some help."

When he stepped out the door a half-hour later, he carried a two-meter rod and a reel, both rented, plus a gooey plastic bag filled with bloodworms. Dan, the owner, had refused to sell him anything but the bait. "Rent for a day, see if you like it. Try the pier maybe, and high tide this evening. Most of those cottages have cleaning tables and fillet knives if you need them."

He felt inflated, equipped for adventure, until he saw the boy squatting near the edge of the parking lot. The boy stared at him, half bored, half sullen, his astonishing coat now twisted and knotted around his waist.

"You know, it doesn't cost much to get one of these," he said to the boy before he really thought about it. "It's supposed to be a good time for flounder . . . I mean he, Dan, said it was. I wouldn't know myself. I could lend you some money."

The boy barely changed his expression, only cracking his mouth, and he saw now why the young face seemed crooked. The boy was missing most of his back teeth on one side. "Naw," he said. "Dan there is my cousin. He'll lend me one after y'all tourists are through. He does me like this all the time." The boy paused to swallow some spit, then opened his jaws in an exaggerated yawn. "I reckon the Lord forgives him even if I don't."

Chris worked his lips but the only sound he managed was a retreating hum. He walked to the car where he carefully laid the twitching rod across the top of both seats. As he dropped the bloodworms into a bag of warm groceries, he reminded himself that he had to stay committed to good sense. Lucy needed him; he was her anchor.

It wouldn't be a good idea to get too involved in anything while he was down here.

That night he retrieved Lucy from the beach. There was no moon, but he was able to locate her with the help of a flashlight he found in a closet. She was delighted to see him, breaking from her statue pose near the foam-threaded surf to smile into his eyes. "It draws us in, doesn't it? So massive and lunar. I didn't want to stay away." He took her hand and led her back across the vertebraed dunes, using the light to scatter the dozens of pale ghost crabs that scuttled underfoot. The dampness of Lucy's skin made him shiver. Later, after her shower, she propped herself on the side of the bed that was closest to the sea. The sliding glass door was open; the wind smelled of salt and insistent storms. Lucy wore nothing but an oversized college sweatshirt that belonged to him, and he watched the perfect furrows of her wet hair leak onto the light fabric, staining it, drying. He wanted her to stay with him, in that bed, until the sun lacquered the water, but knew he couldn't ask for that. She spread her knees, then placed her hands on them in the posture of an elderly, bench-sitting man. "Those crabs are fearless," she said. "Actually unwitting. I stepped on a few of them. They create all that motion in the dark, you know, but I couldn't sense it exactly, though I was trying, wanting to. They pinched me. I crushed them. Instincts worked and failed." She left him then, after a careful kiss on his temple, that place so woven with nerves. The light burned in her bedroom for hours.

He got the car stuck less than a mile down the road to the point. He'd let some air out of the tires to improve traction, but it hadn't helped much. Every other vehicle he saw had four-wheel drive, and he cursed his ignorance until he laughed. What difference did it make? Someone would tow him back to solid ground when the time came. He grabbed the duffel bag, which contained a sandwich, water, a compass, and a camera, then began to follow the rutted road to Hatteras Inlet on foot. Fishermen passed by in their trucks. He lifted a hand without making eye contact. The wind was steady and bracing, and he became aware of the astringent rush of sand past his ankles.

He'd come to see the sites of Fort Hatteras and old Fort Clark, which had once stood across the inlet. There was a historical marker near the ferry dock that mentioned the forts, and it intrigued him, the solemn commemoration of a forgotten skirmish. The makeshift forts had been poorly defended by the Rebels in 1861, but their capture was the first in a series of successes for Union General Ambrose Burnside. Burnside, he knew, eventually rose to lead the Army of the Potomac, guiding it to a smashing defeat at Fredericksburg. He'd always liked the idea that a person's history could be mapped out along lines of success and failure. And he believed it was important, sometimes, to locate even the most blithe points of personal victory. They were easier to forget than the failures. On this day, alone and focused, he planned to tread paths once trod by obscure boots. He would follow the trail of good decisions. He veered off the road when he felt like it and churned through the scorching sand to a low plait of dunes. The morning light had gone silvery like the light that haunted the curves of fine black-and-white photographs.

Nothing. That was exactly what he saw from higher ground, and it was what he'd feared he'd find. There were people scattered up and down the shore, most of them clumped shoulder to shoulder on the point where the fishing was best. There was a small motorboat just beyond the dark bottleneck of the inlet; he could see waves exploding against the chevron of its bow. He wondered what that was like, negotiating the bars and currents of an inlet that had grounded ships for hundreds of years. This had always been the most treacherous part of the Atlantic Coast, defined by the rip of the tides and the assault of the sky. There were no military ruins here. In fact, there was nothing manmade in sight except tire tracks and trash.

The heat rose in layers around him, distorting the landscape, rippling. He imagined a crooked file of fly-ridden troopers, broiling in blue wool, gun barrels untouchable. *Beating double time and struggling and stumbling and finally reaching the weak palisade of Fort Hatteras from behind. It is no contest. The heavy guns aimed at sea cannot turn on them.*

As this vision smoldered, he thought of Lucy and how she wrought words from what eluded her. An afternoon out here—searing, misguided, all but fumbled away—would become a poem for her, a perfect distillation of image and judgment, soaring revelation. Knowing this and feeling it chastise him, he giant-stepped to level ground, then marched toward the probing surf. His wife knew who she was and what she was about more than he ever would. He swung south when his shoes filled with water, determined to circle back to his trapped car only after he'd passed behind every fisherman—and fisherwoman—he could see. He suddenly needed to peer over their bronzed shoulders, smell their bait, note the brand of their beers. He wanted to hear them talk or, more likely, hear them say nothing at all as they faced the task of the sea.

He returned to an empty house. The washer and dryer were running, and the sheets on his bed had been changed. A once-bitten muffin lay sideways on the countertop he'd wiped clean that morning. These were Lucy's little admonitions: she liked things taken care of. He made himself a glass of iced tea and sat to read about the common life of a president, but couldn't concentrate. His back muscles twinged, his stomach rolled. He finally crept down the hall to Lucy's room, where he dug into her jumbled boxes until he found a paperback copy of her second book of poems, the one dedicated to him.

The book still frightened him. She'd written about so much—her divorce, her sister's illness, the decision not to have children—and many of the best poems were about him. How she loved him, yet couldn't do so with all of her heart. How he was sturdy enough to survive the infidelities she confided on other pages, stolid enough not to need the assurance of art. She hadn't turned a blind eye to her own flaws; she was a harsh critic of her ambivalence. Yet he was awed by her ability to make those feelings public. She had taken what was intimate between them and refined it, sharpened its reticent claws, then released it in a flutter of language. She'd crushed and resuscitated them both many times in that book, the one that won prizes, the one that rested on his fingertips with its cover curled like a wilting petal, its margins the color of old teeth. There were passages, mere syllables, that still gutted him though he'd never spoken to Lucy about them, not once. Two affairs? Three? He'd never had the courage to ask.

his is
the flesh of my flesh
unrendered, pallid

There were words he'd never forgotten.

A week later he drove to the Pea Island Wildlife Refuge on the advice of a woman he met on the beach. "They've got nature walks and events like that," she told him, twisting on her towel until her bathing suit slipped to reveal a white crescent of skin. "A good place if you've got some time." He winced as he realized how aimless he must look. She'd never guess he thought about touching that skin beneath her arm. Her children plummeted in and out of the blue-green surf, and he considered inviting her to lunch—with the children, of course. He would drive to a simple restaurant and eat with someone who liked him, who might even admire him. He'd memorize the life in her voice, pay the bill, flirt. But the woman's distracted smile cut him off, so he thanked her and went his way.

The buildings at Pea Island were low, storm-scrubbed slabs that looked as if they belonged next to an oil rig. He stood in the parking lot for several minutes, peering at plastic-shielded maps and reading fine print about the Atlantic Flyway. There were three cars parked near his, and a single government truck. He could see gulls wheeling over the salt marsh, agile and fickle on the wing.

When he went inside, a tall woman in a Fish and Wildlife uniform greeted him from behind a crowded metal desk. Two other women—one gray-haired and large, the other dressed in the waiflike clothes of a student—looked up from where they were scribbling on identical notepads in the far corner of the room.

"You're busy," he said to the ranger. "I'll come back."

The heavy woman in the corner of the room laughed. "If dealing with us keeps Marie busy, she's a worse waste of taxpayer money than I thought. Do your business. Brynna and I are regulars."

"Too regular," grinned Ranger Marie. "At least we're getting work out of you."

"Well then, why don't you tell this gentleman about us. Before you send him up the road to look at your damned fine ospreys."

"Tell him yourself, Helen, and don't scare him off doing it." The ranger gathered a stack of pale blue index cards in her hands. "I've got a bird-watch to lead," she said to him. "Pete will be here in about five minutes to answer any questions you might have about the Refuge. Take a look at our literature, if you like, or let Helen preach on. She used to be with the Church."

"Sisters of Mercy Mild," the heavy woman said, snorting. "But that's another story." She got up from her folding chair and ambled toward him. Her round cheeks were flushed with sunburn, her blue eyes bright and guileless. She wore canvas walking shorts and a T-shirt decorated with a peeling white heron. "We're volunteers here, don't let Marie fool you. Organizing people for the turtle hatch."

The girl, Brynna, flipped her straight hair back over her shoulders. "They're gonna come out soon. It'll be cool."

He looked at the girl more closely. She was perhaps twenty, with large languid eyes, narrow shoulders, a lithe body draped in a gauzy print dress that clung to her thighs. She wore the kind of clunky sandals he hated, and her blunt toes were creased with dirt. He could also see that her brown hair had a purplish tint to it much like

Lucy's did when she used a henna rinse. Recognition of that meaty color against the bones of a stranger's face somehow thrilled him.

"You like turtles?" He wondered if it was possible for him to sound like anyone other than her father. "That must be . . . different."

"Ha," roared Helen, who stood next to him now. "Ha. You take us seriously, mister. Mistake number one. Brynna likes to watch loggerhead nests because it gives her an excuse to spend all night on the dunes with boys."

"That's not fair, Helen," Brynna pouted. "I'm into this as seriously as you are. Pete said he appreciated my commitment."

Helen, however, was still laughing. She wiped her reddened nose with the back of her hand, then clapped that hand onto his shoulder. "If that's not what she's doing out there, she ought to be. It's beautiful work, waiting for a hatch. Also boring as hell."

"I'd like the beauty part," he said.

"I guessed that." Helen flicked her fingers at his chest. "Sign up with Brynna there. This is the week." And she was gone, steering her body gingerly through the doorway and out of sight.

He felt himself blush in the sudden silence. He'd come for exactly this—for connection, to offer his services to an island he was stuck on—but it was suddenly too much. He was about to leave when he noticed Brynna watching him, a yellow pencil twitching in her fingers like a wand.

"The nests up here are really important because the

temperature is, like, cooler than Florida so it makes most of the babies male. Marie was telling me how that happens before you came in. She's really smart, and I like how it's all scientific. I kind of want to be a vet."

"You've done this before?" He slipped his hands into his pants pockets, then yanked them out just as he was about to jingle his loose change.

"Oh, no. I mean this *is* my second summer at Nags Head. I wanted to go to Cape Cod with my friends, but my parents wouldn't let me." She pushed her hair over her shoulder again, a smile lifting half of her mouth. He saw that she had good, straight teeth. "They save a lot of whales up there when they get stuck, you know. I'd like to do that."

He nodded. "Do you think I should sign up? I don't know anything about loggerhead turtles."

"Pete or somebody can tell you that stuff. We just need more people for the early shifts, like four hours or so. Mainly to keep each other awake. There's always time to get the rangers before the babies pop out. They say the sand on top starts to boil, sort of."

"And then you catch them?" He tried to alternate his gaze between her face and a stuffed goose displayed on top of a filing cabinet.

"Oh, no." Her brown eyes went round. "We just make sure they get to the ocean. Before the crabs and birds eat them. Since they're endangered and all."

He signed up to arrive before dusk the next night. "You've got a cool name," Brynna told him, leaning against Marie's desk like a dancer might, hips jutting forward. "You're not a Christopher, which is kind of seriously formal."

"No," he said, measuring his smile, "I'm not."

"You down in Frisco? I work at this sandwich shop—well, it's kind of a bar too—at Mile Post 7."

"I'm in Frisco for a few weeks. My wife is a writer."

Brynna tugged at a smeared, Asian-looking earring. "She writes books? That's neat. I don't do so well in English myself. Get a lot of Cs."

"I was . . . I'm a businessman. We've been married a long time."

"And you love her because she's creative, right? That would be so cool. I went out with this painter guy for a while. He made me feel all beautiful and free. He was really into it."

"Yes, well, Lucy's beyond that now." He had himself look into Brynna's eyes, at her body, while he spoke. "When you get older, work like that is more habit than enthusiasm."

He cooked Lucy dinner. Shrimp cocktail, tuna steaks, white wine he'd brought from home. She ate every bite and sat on his lap later as they watched the pocked moon rise over the water. He did all that he could to keep his mind in the present moment, to appreciate the unique accretions of his marriage. It was simply a matter of breathing from within, he told himself, of going deep, much like Lucy did when she was practicing yoga. Although as he looked at his wife's neck and saw the creped skin there, he realized it had been a long while since he'd seen her doing yoga or anything of the kind.

Just when he was sure she'd fallen asleep in his arms, she asked if she could read to him. It irritated him to know she'd folded against him, body pliant as a child's, while her mind was elsewhere. He kept his eyes closed as she slipped down the hall for her notebooks, though he listened closely for the sound of her feet on carpet, then wood, anticipating the swift percussion of each step. When she sat in the armchair across from him and began to speak, he searched her voice for hints of artifice or condescension or doubt. But it was as if she were speaking to him from the expanding chambers of her heart, aligning all that mattered to her into the verses of song. There was no hint of a retreating, jealous God. She spoke of durable love instead, the sunrise, the sea. She described the low, awkward flight of pelicans. She recast a story he'd once told her about betraying his brother in a ball game many years before, and her version, while brief, became true. She sounded small and honest and warm to him, careful, and it was this he loved along with the wind-softened crash of the ocean. It was this that carried him to sleep.

He was paired with Helen, and he didn't believe the pairing was an accident. Brynna was to go with a sun-dried old man who'd brought binoculars even though it was dusk. The old man was quizzing Brynna closely, asking if she'd want some soda crackers or cheese during the night, when Brynna caught his eye and gave him an exaggerated wink. He was too surprised to wink back.

He squeezed himself into the rear of Pete's government-issue Blazer while Helen settled in front, her legs so large he could see them on either side of her seat. She began a monologue. "I bet you'd come when I first saw you. Told that to Marie but she wouldn't take the odds, said I should stick to bingo like that was a funny thing to say. Ha. I did go to the racetrack some when I was at St. Joe's. I liked it. All that praying for luck without going through God first. All that ridiculous hope. Though the ponies had nothing to do with me leaving the church. No, sir."

He decided he wouldn't ask her why she'd left, no matter what.

"It was the bird-watching, to tell the truth." She rubbed the convex tops of her thighs. "At Cape May, then down here. I told the bishop I couldn't give it up. Now the rest of them are stuck inside, jealous as hell of my Life List."

He knew enough not to believe her. And he understood she was trying to find out whether he was going to be sheepish or combative, whether he'd admit his real reason for coming. Pete, a laconic high-hatted ranger, wasn't interested in mediating between them. He didn't interrupt to talk about turtles or habitat preservation or the erosion near Oregon Inlet Bridge. "Nice night," he said, glancing at Chris in the bulky rearview mirror. "I like going out on a nice night."

Pete dropped them off, and they walked the short distance to the beach where they settled into the sun-warmed palm of a dune. The nest was perhaps twenty feet behind them, a staked-out depression in the sand surrounded by reverential footprints.

"I've been thinking about you," Helen said, unscrewing the noisy cap of a canteen. "Wondering if you're an artist, like Brynna says your wife is, or what. Want to help me on that?"

"I ran a business in Connecticut. I'm retired."

"A businessman? That tells me exactly nothing. Very WASPy of you to say it that way." She paused to drink. "So you're saying you don't write like your wife? How's it go then—you worship the little words she puts together?"

He swung his head around. Helen's eyes were stark in the final rinse of twilight. "Yes," he said, "I'd say that's precisely how it goes."

She sighed and dug into a hip pocket. He heard the insistent crackle of cellophane and thought about his voice, how it sounded cool and formal in his ears. "I'm nosy, I know," Helen continued. "I like to pick at people from their blind side, which is another technique I stole from my lousy past life. But I figure she's either famous, which makes you feel inadequate. Or she's not, and she hates that, so she *makes* you feel inadequate. You can't win with artist types. Though I ought to confess I think it's impossible to win with any type at all."

"You're a cynic on top of everything else?" He tried a dry chuckle. "Maybe we should slow down here and arrange a truce, talk some about turtles."

"We could, but that's dull." She'd stuffed her mouth with cookies, and her munching was jovial, irritating. "I want to know what makes you tick. I'm curious. Do you believe in love? America? Is your wife faithful to you? Stuff like that."

He imagined quiet, a meditation that would become as perfect as the pitch of the wind that sang through the sea oats above them—perfect and unwavering. Instead this woman was buzzing in his ears, angering him, and he could feel something cresting inside him, a thing he'd lived with for a long time. It rose upward to his voice, like dark treasure on the tide.

"You want to know what I really think of Lucy? After all these years, these . . . retreats?" He began to stand, then sat again, amazed by his own motion. He could sense Helen's eyes on him, fixed and guarded. "What if I said she's selfish and loveless and hollow? That she's all fragments. Cutting. Would you stop talking, if I said . . . if I . . . exaggerate?" He swallowed. There was more. He felt the lines of words racing along his tongue, spurred on by guilt and fear.

"Got you going, didn't I?" Helen's voice—toneless, bullying.

"No," he said, beginning a slow slide down the gritty slant of the dune. "I'm capable of that myself."

He stood and veered into the night feeling shivery, raw. A tantrum, he told himself. That's what it had been. He'd walk, whisk his head clean. But he'd gone less than half a mile when he ran into Brynna, who'd been at a nesting site just up the beach. "I knew it was you," she said, skirts blown like bracken around her pale legs. "I could tell, like it was a little bit psychic almost. Marie wanted me to get you guys. It's crazy up there, these turtlets are everywhere, and that old guy I'm with is going nuts, keeping us back like he's the official guard or something. He even elbowed me in the boobs he's so into it, then didn't notice enough to apologize. God."

"I'm sorry," he said.

"You would be."

He reached for her upper arm, pretending to steady himself against it, winded. The milky beams of several flashlights were visible against the inland sky as though what was happening there was a marquee event, some kind of ocean premiere. Behind him, back up the invisible beach, there were no glimmers or winks. Nothing.

"Want to go see?" Brynna shifted her weight against his in a playful shove. "You might not want to miss something so cool in Nature. With Man helping out and not hurting things like we always do."

"I'm fine," he said, wondering how he might undress her in his scorched mind. He wanted to be woozy enough to idealize her, to believe she'd be a relief. "I'd rather stay here. Talk with a lovely lady like you."

"Oh. Sure. Yeah." She smiled and her good teeth looked almost horsey in the rime light that rode the water. "Guys like you always want to talk."

Lucy was waiting for him when he returned to the cottage. She was drawn into a tight ball on the couch, arms locked around her knees. Her hair was a mess, and her eyes darted right and left between their lids as if they were looking for an escape. He thought to himself, *My wife has nothing but this.* He began to speak. She cut him off.

"Why don't you treat me like I'm Thorazined?" she croaked. "Do me that favor."

"Lucy?" Her name a whisper—the best he could do.

"Where have you been?"

"On the beach. With the turtles. I told you about it."

"I went deaf, Chris. I couldn't hear a sound. No words, no scratches. And you weren't here. He's not here!" She screeched into the white valley of skin between her knees.

"I *am* here." He was drawn across the floor, a thin, scarred ache in his chest. "I was with some people. I didn't know you—"

"You were with someone else? You need to torture me with that?"

"I had an ugly conversation with a nun, that's all. An ex-nun."

"Did you fuck her? Did you want to?"

"Lucy!" She was as strung out as he'd ever seen her. Although it occurred to him that even this might be some kind of wretched test. "You've had a bad time," he said. "We'll work it out . . . ." His words trailed off.

"There are others. I can smell them because I'm a madwoman just now, the insane mute bitch you married. Did you screw her, whoever she was, so young and sure of herself? Just tell me that."

"No," he said. And he hadn't. Although he'd wanted to. He'd wanted to take Brynna, who'd only let him kiss her, and make her understand the consequences of her naiveté, her jellied ignorance. He'd walked the beach for hours after leaving her, his clothes whipping like flags against his body. He'd been so many men on that journey. Husband, lover, soldier, inventor, frontier priest in a cassock torn to rags. Lucy refused to see that about him. How he could imagine and change. How he had mystery.

"Don't lie to me, Chris. It reminds me of Mark."

"I'm not lying. And I'm nothing like Mark. Please don't start down that road."

"I will." She pounded the couch cushion with an opened hand. "I will. Neither of you understands what this costs me. I try to find this . . . these . . . ." Her hoarse voice went nowhere. ". . . and you're too busy disrupting things. I need you at home."

It began again—the old feelings falling into place. He loved her, he'd nestle her, she'd come around. But when he drew himself together to kiss the tangled crown of her head, he couldn't do it. The image was still there: his legs striding, his nostrils filling with wild, invisible air.

"I want to be here for you. Until you're all right."

"I'm never all right," she sobbed. "I've abandoned too much."

He walked on and away. As he passed Lucy's room, he remembered some of the poems she had read to him the night before. . . . *shell of cannon, shell of bone* . . . Torrents of description. *Gulf Stream, hissing, snaked* . . . . A sequence she hoped to craft into a long poem about this rough coast. She wanted the beauty and the danger, the history and the yearning, transformed into words. He paused for a moment to listen; her sobs were rhythmic and shallow, the hiccups of an aggrieved child. He knew the sound. What mattered were Lucy's tribulations, and that was what she wrote her life upon—her failures and the failures she insisted upon others.

He slept until early afternoon, a sweating but dreamless sleep. When he sat up in bed he realized that the clatter of blinds had awoken him, not sunlight, or even his powerful, gagging thirst. Blinds were clanging and knocking everywhere. The sliding door in his room had been opened, and as he limped into the hallway, he saw that all of the doors and windows in the house were open, curtains pulled back, screens removed. One look in Lucy's room revealed that the miniature chaos of her labors had been cleared away. No books, no papers, no wrinkles on the beds. He thought at first, with a surprised leaping in his chest, that she'd left him. But as he moved into the crosscurrents of the living room, he saw a tidy stack of her belongings near the couch and became less wary. If he'd learned anything the night before, it was that she needed him in the most mundane, pummeling ways.

There was a piece of paper on the counter in the kitchen. Handwritten, creased in the middle as though it had been folded only to be unfolded again, it was held in place by a seashell and a deck of playing cards he'd bought but never opened. A poem, one he'd never seen. Memories of all she had kept from him—the lovers, the gods, the ghosts—twisted hard along his spine, yet he couldn't resist. He stood in the rattling, wind-stripped room and read the poem, then read it again. It claimed, in a language more lovely and terse than he could speak, that he would forgive her, always forgive her, because it was his lot and his heart. They were twined together, throttling, and he could not resist.

Semper Paratus

We were a good boat crew. A lot better than anything I saw in boot camp, which you would hope was true. We drilled, ran constant checks on our equipment. We had to. There were only seven of us assigned to the station—a station with an Area of Responsibility of 1,350 miles—and we had hundreds of pleasure craft and beaucoup bad weather to deal with. That made it a choice billet for me. Much better than galley duty on the cutter *Harriet Lane,* which was where I started. At Station Ocracoke, I had what I wanted: plenty of contact with boats and water. I can't speak for the guys. We were all after different things in our careers and our lives, and maybe we still are.

I'd been with Group Cape Hatteras two months, working on promotion to petty officer, when I drew a three-week rotation on Ocracoke Island. James Leggett was our Boatswain's Mate. I believed I could deal with him. He'd been supervisor on crews with women before.

He was career and steady and stuck to his business. The kind of guy you wanted to kid about officer school, tell him he needed to get his lieutenant's stripes so he could kick some Academy ass. He'd gnaw on a laugh if you said that, then shake his blondish head. He liked taking the Coast Guard at an enlisted man's pace.

Leggett knew how to run things. Burgoyne, our Machinery Tech, was slick with engines and every other piece of metal in the harbor. Like a lot of shop rat MTs, Burgoyne kept to himself when he could. So did I. The crew accused me of studying all the time, then they'd ask why I bothered, every apprentice seaman from here to Alaska knew I didn't have to bust it for promotion, promotions were handed to women like candy. I ignored the shots like I was supposed to. It was basic shit, part of our lazy downtime talk about R&R and money. The shit that meant something was stowed underneath our work blues. Where it was safest.

Those weeks at Ocracoke it was me, Leggett, Burgoyne, Paul Toshiko, Trey Buckner, Lyle Pozek, and Sammy Walker. There were five other women at Hatteras, but I was the only one who pulled the straw. Which didn't concern me, like I said. I can eat anything a guy cooks, and I know how to be good crew. I was sure we'd catch some hardcore Search-and-Rescue on Ocracoke, the stuff that makes my blood run best. There'd be no dry rot for us.

Buckner and Pozek asked me out to play pool at the Jolly Roger the afternoon we transferred down. They'd done their calculating and rank toting and knew we'd be hitting the waves together. I was senior to them both, though not by much. We needed to be able to look each other in the eye. I'm a lousy pool player. So is Pozek, who's not much good at anything he's not made to focus on. Buckner shoots a mean game and likes to hip-slide around the corners of the table like he's on a waxed dance floor even when there aren't any girls to impress. A shimmy, Pozek calls it . . . as in *Shimmy for me, Buck.* At least once a day Buckner tells me—and everybody else—that he can't wait to finish his hitch, he should've been a marine. He's got restlessness like it's a four-season allergy. Makes him a ball-slamming shooter though, all focus and heat, just like it can make him awesome on drills. His body knows how to burn unhappiness for fuel.

So we're playing Cut Throat and I'm doing all right and the Jolly Roger is empty except for a couple of kids eating french fries in a back corner that smells like trapped crab. The jukebox is looping through some old Trisha Yearwood songs, Pozek's choice. We've got time to bitch about our assignment, but we don't, maybe because I don't feel like clipping Buckner's claws when he gets snotty, which he will. I've got this feeling it's better if we stay quiet on the subject. Then Leggett walks in, all broad shoulders and regulation. I can tell by the stoked way he moves in from the black square of the door that he knew we'd be here. He orders a Coke, comes over to the table. Lyle, he says, Trey, Randall. Using my last name like they all do. Pozek invites him into the game but he says no, not this time. He'll just stand by. Leggett is a watcher, we all know that. Question is, what's the man, our superior, hope to see?

Some cold coast in Michigan—that's where Leggett is from. He told me once that seeing the big cutters on the Great Lakes did him in as a kid, worse than a junior high romance. The Coast Guard kissed him hard. Tonight, he seems so keyed his voice drags on a drawl I haven't heard before, and I hear him talk to Buckner about a mutual friend of theirs who's a Tech on the Hatteras buoy tender. The friend has racked up some negatives with the chief. Pozek then has to go goofing on me, doing the male-dog thing that guys do to get attention when they outnumber the girls in a room even if the girls aren't ones they're thinking about screwing, not with the front part of their brains. He tells Leggett I suck as a pool player, it's a good thing I toss line better than I slide a stick. He says it every way he can to make Leggett laugh. Which doesn't happen. Then it's my turn, and I can feel Leggett surveying my back, casting a shadow between my shoulders. I miss a semi-tough shot on the (11) ball. Pozek slaps the rail of the table. Buckner nails me with his brown eyes, which always go darker around the edge when there's a Boatswain or anyone else close by who might call his number. Buckner looks at me and shrugs, turning away to the bar to get a refill for his beer. Yeah, his eyes say, Randall sucks at pool and everything else outside the system. What else is new?

I spend a little time—like three seconds—trying to

frame up why Buckner might have it in for me, then I drop it. We all have our moods.

Then something about the satisfied way Pozek is chewing his bottom lip takes me back to recruit training at Cape May. My Company Commander never made a face like that; CC was never satisfied. But there was a girl in my company—name was Yancy Treet from some pothole town near St. Louis—who practiced twisting her brown mouth that way. She was in the Guard to get a government job and keep it. Don't waste your blood heat on a paycheck. Don't pretend. Yancy liked to tell me how she was going to wait out all the bullshit boat procedure, how soon she'd be behind a desk forever. Snacking on her busy lip. Last I heard she was a seaman on the *Mohawk* down in the Florida Keys, collecting Haitians from Lincoln Log rafts and sailing them away from fenced-in America.

We finished up our game when Buckner sank two cracking bank shots on the ② and the ⑤. Leggett left before that. As he hit the door he told me he'd see me whenever. His mouth was as straight as a ruler, and his left hand cupped the knobby bone above his fresh-shaved neck, a thing it always did when he was thinking hard. He was making the effort, I could see that. But it was still true he was fighting to keep things even between us. I'd noticed it for a couple of weeks, ever since I spliced a moor line on a drill and turned to see him memorizing me. It was like an uncorked smell in the air, rank and sweet at the same time. Temptation.

We both recognized it. And being old hands, we knew better than to do anything about it.

I was driving and Buckner asked me to stop at the store so he could get cigarettes, which I did. Pozek went with him just to wander the aisles and flirt with the high schooler pecking at the cash register. A few of our guys play up the sailors-in-a-port attitude, acting like their haircuts and wrapped-in-plastic dress uniforms mean something. But we aren't navy. That gets drilled into our heads in boot camp and beyond. For us, there isn't ever any shore leave, not like the swabbies have it. Maybe at the air stations, yeah, where we have pilots and jump-suit officers, but not in these tiny harbor towns. *Semper paratus*. You don't shit in your own nest. If Buckner and Pozek wanted to screw around, they'd be smart to go way up the beach to Nags Head to do it.

Me, I liked to go even further. When I had the chance.

So we got to the station without much talking, though Buckner, at least, seemed to think he'd checked something off his list by including me in the game. The way he said good night dropped him just short of being a full-bird asshole. I went to the prefab I had all to myself, finished unpacking, sat on my bunk for a while trying to decide which manuals I was most likely to read. At 2200 the klaxon rang for the Motor Lifeboat crew to respond to a foundering cabin cruiser a mile southeast of the inlet. The call went well. We were able to bail the cruiser with the portable pump before we escorted her in. I was asleep fifteen minutes after I went off watch.

We'd served most of our stint before the bad thing happened. It was early spring, the days were clearing off in twos and threes, but we'd seen gale-force winds a couple of times, taken ten to twelve calls. This is why I can say our crew was good. We'd handled some tricky stuff, including a night tow of a ketch through Teach's Hole. We weren't cocky. That's not a feeling any of us believed we could afford. But we knew how to make certain kinds of decisions together. So it's hard, even now, to bring it all into focus. Parts are as clear as can be. I can run them like high-resolution video behind my eyes again and again, even though visibility was poor near the end because of the darkness and the storm. I've got stark mental snapshots I have to live with. What I don't have is enough peace or logic. If there are such things.

Sammy Walker was standing watch when the call got relayed. An inshore charter scooting down the sound with the tide, out late like they sometimes are if they want to catch mullet for bait, spots what looks like an empty skiff banging off the lee side of a dredge island southeast of Howard Reef. The captain calls it in. He can't get close enough to see much. The sandbars there are crazy, especially at ebb tide. Plus, the wind is kicking pretty good, he's got it at twenty or twenty-five knots out of the north. He thinks we ought to take a look. Sammy gets a position, asks if the captain sees any other craft in the area, but the captain gives a negative on that. Sammy rings in Leggett, shows him the chart that puts the skiff's position close to the northern border of our

AOR. Leggett orders up a crew for the Rigid Hull Inflatable, the position is way too shallow for the Motor Lifeboat. That's when we got our bell. Three minutes after the call. Three more minutes and we've suited up and cast off, leaving Burgoyne, Toshiko, and Walker to man the fort.

Some good news, some not so good. We had fifteen or twenty minutes of daylight left, mostly because the weather was clear to the west and we were catching a lot of reflected sun off a hanging cloud bank. But the barometer was dropping, and that northern wind was as fresh as the charter captain said. We took it full in the face as soon as we changed course out of Big Foot Slough Channel. Sammy radioed us with two bits of information. One was that Station Hatteras had been called out on a possible Gulf Stream collision and the air station at Elizabeth City was pitching in on that, so everybody was tied up. We might not be able to snag a 'copter if we decided to look for floaters. Second was the report of a squall headed right down the coast, hard rain, winds over forty knots. None of it bothered Leggett, who was at the wheel as our cox. What bothered him was how the tide was running with the wind, which meant a man overboard, if that's what we had, would be damn hard to find in the dark.

We rode in silence, catching plenty of stinging spray off the bow, each thinking our own thoughts. Buckner loved Search-and-Rescue as much as I did. Seated portside in his dry suit, helmet, and vest, he was dog alert, nose in the air. Both hands were fisted together between his knees. I was stationed as lookout just off the starboard bow, my fingers clove-hitched in anticipation. Pozek was in the stern, close enough to Leggett to hear him without shouting.

I thought about the possibilities, arranging my ideas in checklists and columns as I imagined Leggett, or any good Boatswain, would. I didn't think about how well Leggett wanted me to perform on calls, how that seemed to vent his steam some, seeing me do well. I dodged that thought as I had before. I figured a tourist wouldn't be out in a skiff this early in the year; I wanted to think the person or persons connected were natives smart enough to wear life jackets and have good habits. An old hand working his crab pots. Or laying nets for mullet. Though most of the locals got off the water for their suppers when they could. Engine trouble, maybe. There ought to be oars aboard, however, unless the operator was a fool. Truth be told, I didn't like my tally. Either the skiff had been abandoned and some lazy bastard had failed to notify us like he was supposed to, or the occupant was in the water, maybe hurt, maybe not.

We passed our first cluster of dredge isles as last light drained away. Because the Banks are so unstable, summer dredges have to suck sand from the channels and spit it into piles to keep things passable. And we weren't into summer yet. There were sandbars scattered like thrown rice on the backside of Ocracoke. Leggett knew the subsurface well, though. We'd run it enough in recent days.

And he was counting on me to keep my eyes peeled in the bow. He throttled back the diesel when he had to, waiting for my read on the chop.

We sighted the charter boat who'd made the call at 2007. Without a dinghy aboard, she'd been able to do little but stand by with her lights ablaze. Leggett swung us to starboard, then idled the engine about a hundred feet off her stern. Instructions from Sammy put the skiff near a steep bank of dredged sand, maybe three hundred yards east. Pozek stood spread-legged beside our Boatswain and aimed a light. Sure enough, she was there. Low in the water and white as hot metal in our beam. Buckner, who had binoculars, shouted off her registration, what little he could see with her gunwales so low. Leggett called it in as he gave us enough throttle to counter the pulling tide. He also radioed the charter captain to ask if he'd seen or heard anything. He hadn't.

The idea was to slide in above the skiff and secure her first. The RHI is plenty maneuverable, especially in good hands, but there was still a chance one or two of us would have to go into the water. The charts showed depths of one to four feet, but we all knew how to be skeptical about the charts, especially after a hard winter. If the skiff wasn't anchored, we'd need to steady her for a search, then proceed from there.

Buckner saw the bow line when I did, a tight thread dropping straight off the prow, and we both agreed the skiff might be anchored fore and aft, which would account for her being swamped in the chop. Leggett ordered out the tow line and bridle anyway. I got them ready. He put the diesel in neutral, gave me the order to hail and go board as we came alongside. Pozek was still bleaching everything with his light. We caught some rogue swells coming in, however, and that caused our first bit of trouble.

Buckner was supposed to grab the craft midship and make fast a line while I boarded. And that's what he started to do. But he heard something, he said later, something animal and pained. We clipped the skiff pretty hard making our approach in the swells. Maybe that was Leggett's mistake. But he didn't know what we had out there, none of us did. And the rain had started to come at us in needles. What we'd done was knock the kid loose from the starboard side of the skiff.

I was in the swamped craft, about to run my regs. Check for onboard survivors. Check anchor lines. Check fuel leaks. But Buckner came aboard right behind me and was out again, overboard in at least five feet of rough water before I could turn and cuss him out. He claimed he shouted before he went in, but I don't remember that. What I remember is Pozek's huge white moon of a light and how it shielded me from the dark spar of Leggett as Buckner busted procedure and took matters into his own hands.

The asshole went in without orders or a line. He figured it was shallow enough and he said he could actually breathe that kid's fear, it rushed into his lungs and head before he even processed it. Like a grab for a falling baby, he told me later. He shouted to Leggett, *Man in, Man in.* He did do that when he surfaced, and we knew right away we had more than a floater. But I had to tie off the lines Buckner had neglected first. I had to. Meanwhile, Leggett ordered Pozek off the light and into the skiff with me, life buoy in hand. This was good crew. Buckner left a blank, Pozek filled it. I didn't have time to look at Pozek's face, what little was visible beneath his helmet, but I didn't have to see his full black eyes to know he was still calm, still greased and ready.

Unlike Buckner. He was so damn sure his strong body could fix this one. He pushed the prow of the skiff backward—I felt the shove—then went under for the kid. No lights, the kid was struggling to grab the skiff, weighed down by the damn waders put on to check nets, unable to get out of the waders because an ankle was wedged—and broken—in the rusty, shitty mass of rebar that made up the guts of the dredge island. The same rebar that had fouled the kid's nets in the first place. Buckner got the kid up for air, shouting for assistance, saying the kid was trapped, cut the nets, cut the nets. He thought the kid was wrapped up that way. I went in on Leggett's order, clear of Buckner and his armful of thrashing. Pulled my light. Spit out a high, cold slap of surf. My eyes burned with the first rinse of salt, but I saw Buckner's wide mouth moving under the orange cup of his helmet, repeating something soft and calm I couldn't hear. The kid was still alert enough to cough some. I saw that, too. Then came another rank of swells, God damn Pozek and Leggett for not seeing they needed to clear off. The water surged in over us and brought the skiff right at Buckner's head.

He took the kid down. Heave to, I screamed, back off. Leggett saw my waving arms and hauled the diesel into reverse, gave me as much room as the skiff's anchor lines would allow. Now that I was in the water, I could feel how bad and strange it was to be caught in the yanking backwash. The surf was hammering. My feet searched for purchase on the chunked concrete. I could touch bottom every few seconds but it didn't last. It took Pozek too long to realize he had to cut the skiff's lines and get the damn thing out of there. Too long. Holding the useless life buoy in position, he seemed to want the order relayed through Leggett, who was fighting the wheel, as though he couldn't hear the words any other way. I had to tell him twice. I went under with my light until I could see the huddled shape that made up Buckner and the kid. He was waiting until he was sure it was safe. When the skiff was finally towed free, I signaled Buckner with my light. He powered up with the kid wrapped in his arms. God damn, Randall, he shouted between gulps of air. You gotta cut this kid free.

But it wasn't the nets. I went down and found the foot clamped between iron and rock. Cut away some mesh, I did that. Cut away the waders. Living all the time in the single-tone roar of the undersea. No go, I told Buckner, no go. All gasping and spit. Let me relieve. We were doing it on our own now, together, caged by rain and waves, Buckner squeezing water out of the kid's lungs, or trying to, me diving less than five feet, not able to shift the rebar, taking the kid from Buckner's rimrock arms, the transfer gentle even with the froth and breakers. That's a snapshot I have: spikes of black hair around a child's white face. We all look more like children when we're that soaked and cold. I worked that kid. Floated her, kept her head up, kissed her with mouth-to-mouth, wiped the vomit. I felt what Buckner hadn't felt, the berry breasts under my clamping forearm. Not that it mattered. Buckner tried like hell to rip her free. I'm gonna cut him, he said, shooting up for air. Tell me to cut his ankle, Randall, it's our only chance. His eyes were round and glazed like they get when we run through our adrenaline into the sledge of exhaustion. He was gagging salt water but didn't seem to know it. Another shot I have: savage, demanding Buckner. Leggett was thirty yards away, bucking the RHI in the surf. But Buckner wasn't looking for orders, he was looking for a way. No, I said. You get the tow line from Leggett and you pull that rebar free. We'll all pull. Now.

We were so different. That fact took hold like a death grip right then, and it nearly stopped us both. I was the best one on the crew for him to work with—he knew it, he damn well did—but it made Trey Buckner hate me. I was the one who reeled his crazy, muscled self in, and he never hated me more than then. The hate welded a new color into his full-flushed eyes. I hated him, too. He'd fucked procedure from the word go. But it was a good hate, hot and furious in that night water, and it gave us what we needed to try and save that kid.

Leggett was trying to keep the inflatable from being beaten ashore, trying to sort out what was happening in the water. Buckner stroked out and signed to Pozek for the gear. It was a long shot. The RHI might not have enough power, especially running against the current. But it was a chance. Burgoyne babied that engine. I was sure I could feel the kid shiver against me while I held her, I believed that. It wasn't too late. Buckner rigged the line right beneath us, then gave Pozek the thumb. I did what I had to do, cradled that girl against a pillow of concrete so I could shield her from the waves. Buckner dove to rip at the rebar with his hands. He was frantic now, though I only knew that from the sandpapering of his breath. He no longer yelled or wasted motion.

Tore the kid free, that's what he did. Somebody later told me the whole operation took a little over fifteen minutes. It's a slo-mo distortion I don't need to relive. The inside of the kid's foot was peeled out of its skin, half of Buckner's fingers, even with gloves, were no better. It didn't matter. We couldn't revive her. Not with Pozek and Leggett working fresh. Not with the airlift thirty minutes later. We broke her ribs, her sternum, never got her back. Sixteen years old from a longtime island family, she'd gone to pull nets for an ailing grandfather. Not the first drowning they'd suffered, I was told. Probably not the last.

For me, either. Or any of us. I'd pulled floaters before,

but I'd never lost a live one. I thought I knew enough not to let her haunt me. Part of this job demands coping with being too late. I think of frost-faced Yancy Treet when I think of that. Then there are the mistakes. Did you make them? Can you admit them? Do you blame a man—or a woman—for not acting the way you think you might? Do you *want* them to act the same? Buckner tortured himself over that girl's death, claimed he knew her from the ice-cream shop or some place like that even though we knew it wasn't true. He believed what he wanted to believe. That we could have done it. I'm not so sure. You don't get to pick your water or your weather out here, and you don't get fair chances. *Always ready.* That's our responsibility, and it's the only responsibility I'll ever swear by, in the Coast Guard or out. You don't get to find your luck in this life. You have to be prepared for anything, including the worst.

Leggett kept us together for the next few days. That was his job, and he did it. He gave us no time to think or brood. The calls kept coming. We kept responding. *Semper, semper.* A small yacht ran aground because the skipper was drunk and stupid. A trawler out of Wanchese was reported overdue. A ferry had engine trouble. The Hyde County Sheriff passed on a tip about marijuana being smuggled through the harbor by some sailboat yuppies. I worked the girl's loss out of my system like soreness out of my muscles. I made it a physical matter. Things went blank between me and Leggett, though. He wide-eyed me, but it wasn't the same. It was like the failure with the girl—which we didn't talk about except officially—and the forgiveness—which we somehow owed each other—froze all channels between us. He didn't write Buckner up for jumping the gun, that may have been a scrap thrown my way. I don't know. It was a while before we could pass each other in the hallways or on the docks like normal people, no shuttered faces, no stops and starts, and then it was all right. The scent trail was gone.

Pozek was another matter. He went big-sister pissed at Buckner, rabbit-punching him with fake newspaper headlines to make him mad. *Selfless Rescue Swimmer Fails. USCG Witness to Teen Drowning.* But Pozek had nothing to say to me. He knew he should have reacted faster when he was on the skiff, but he couldn't be sure his screwup had made any difference. Instead of running the scenario over and over in his head, sanding it down to livable, he tried to scrape his way into Buckner's thick hide, which was the exact wrong place to be.

With me and Buckner it was more complicated. We developed a thundercloud survivor's bond, all gloom and hovering. He still called me Randall, and it wasn't a friendship in any way. Not one. It wasn't a sex thing either though we had to try that, with Buckner's stiff, scabbed hands, to know it. We didn't shoot pool anymore and had only one halfway regular conversation over warm coffee and that was mostly about his growing up in South Carolina with a son-of-a-bitch dad and how he was no longer in touch with any of his brothers.

What we had between us was the dirty fact we fit together when things were dire and messed up. And only then. I could see how he wanted another dose of it, Buckner did. But not by talking about what happened or about that girl, Karla Wahab. I'll bet he didn't mouth the syllables of her name more than once, even when he was cutting himself up about her death. What he wanted was more rage and swimming. A merciless heart pounding harder than the merciless surf. Risk. Blind rescue. I'd been there with him, and he knew I wanted it, too.

I meant to tell Pozek that what we'd been through wasn't worth it. Even after he lay down hints about my body like he was some kind of jealous when all Buckner and I had gained was one fuck and coping. Who wants deafness and loss of speech, the inability to communicate with anything except a sea you can't change? Except telling Pozek that would have been a lie. I thought of those castaway moments when I polished brass in the stale, mosquitoed harbor. I'd riptide into daydreams about them, surrounded by men as I was. Buckner and I truly could not bear each other, not in orgasm or chore, but we had found the pitiless, unwinnable world we all imagine. All know. And it was, in ways I didn't yet understand, the world we'd clearly trained for.

Brother, Unadorned

The sky above the inlet went waterline gray, and the captain complained about the drainsuck of the tide until most of us voted to go back to port. My brother, Mitch, wanted to stay out. He'd brought good rain gear, and cold never bothered him much—my memories of him feature wind-slapped cheeks and tireless eyes—but he didn't argue. He gave the flounder he'd caught to a bony, chalk-faced boy wearing an Orioles cap and spent the return trip in the bow, leaning forward as if he were waiting for something to flash free of the turbulent water. Porpoise maybe. Or a raggedy cormorant.

I stayed in the cabin at first, huddled on a cooler that didn't belong to me. The boat's radio squawked and twanged. Two men from Raleigh shared black coffee and pretzels with the rest of us. Captain, however, was reluctant to give up center stage. He seemed to know that talk among his customers would eventually lead to talk about him, and he'd already suffered a lousy morning. So he continued his ribald monologue about fish, fishing equipment, and dumb tourists until everyone's chuckle sounded hollow. I snuck out between the covered bait wells and took up a solitary position in the stern, where I watched a dark-haired man walk across the roughened silver of the flats to check his nets. He wore chest-high waders, and his boat was a crescent of smoky shadow anchored into the wind. I wondered what my brother was thinking, forty feet ahead of me, up there in the unsheltered salt spray. I wondered how we'd spend the day, *our* day, now that the fishing trip had been canceled.

The wind was lighter and drier in the harbor, but the *Miss Hatteras* emptied quickly. Mitch helped the mate gather buckets and torn gobbets of bait and told him to keep the six-pack of German beer we'd brought. He also tipped the kid. The boat hadn't been out much more than an hour; I could tell the kid wasn't expecting money. But Mitch was good at being kind, always had been, especially when he wasn't under any pressure. He gave a ten-dollar bill to the mate, and he wasn't hasty or sneaky like men who've finally come upon money in their lives usually are. He held the bill out calmly, pressed flat between his palm and thumb as if he were purchasing a gift, a thing he'd really thought about.

We walked along the quay toward my Jeep, Mitch in front. A Gulf Stream charter churned through the mouth of the harbor to our right. "You don't think this was a bust, do you?" I said. "You're not mad."

"No, ma'am." He paused to rub his neck against the stiff collar of his slicker. "I needed that."

"What? A dose of bad weather?"

"Ocean sounds and stuff. A little peace, even if it's just a little. You know what I mean."

I squeezed past a listing fuel tank and unlocked the Jeep. "Yeah, I guess I do," I said, stuffing our duffel bags inside, "and the hell of it is you've got all day to tell me about it anyway."

We were quiet in the car, however. The ways we spoke to one another had been nearly forgotten, like the lyrics to pre-school songs. Except for brief family vacations such as this one, Mitch and I hadn't lived in the same house for almost fifteen years. He didn't have to answer my prickly challenges anymore. He had a wife who challenged him. And a child. And a growing number of patients. When we spoke on the telephone, a perfunctory holiday trick, I could hear him receding from me when I asked a question. He would fade—or sink—into the life he lived there in Williamsburg, his voice barely fluent in the language of goodwill.

So why did I care? We were at the age when siblings are either a comfort or they are nothing at all. We no longer had to share our clothes, our jealousies. I told myself I should be grateful for the space. My longtime boyfriend, Brian, had done little but snipe at me the past six months, insisting I was muzzled and preoccupied, as overlayered as the walls of the Monument Avenue townhouse we were restoring. Then he moved out. It seemed that part of me wanted to be left alone. But another part, the more timid half, wanted to visit the shrines of old affections.

I pulled the Jeep into the parking lot of the Red & White. Mitch got out and started putting air in the tires before I had a chance to ask him to. I went inside and bought two steaks, two Idaho potatoes, a bag of kettle-cooked chips, and some ice cream. Our parents were on Ocracoke Island. Our brother Paul was hang gliding on Jockey's Ridge. Mitch's wife, Liz, had taken the baby to visit college friends in Nags Head. They'd all be gone until after dinner, so I decided to skip the seafood and imported green vegetables. I thought we should do what we damn well pleased, the way we'd once claimed we would.

I found Mitch petting a scrawny Chesapeake Bay retriever in the cord grass next to the pay phones. It was a bitch, sunburned, wedge-headed, her webbed feet nicked with scars. She was already in love with my brother.

He didn't even look up at me. "I always wanted one of these. You remember that, the guy in Coinjock selling puppies out of his truck? I begged Dad until I cried." He ran his nimble surgeon's fingers across the dog's belly. She squirmed with pleasure. "Closest I ever got was half-share of a mutt in med school. This one doesn't have a collar, she's starving. What do you think? Cece will go crazy if I bring her home."

I squeezed the bag of groceries to my chest, feeling the cool, firm pads of the steaks through the brown paper. I remembered the dry-lipped kiss my sister-in-law had given Mitch that morning before we stepped out the door, the way she frowned at me. "Liz is the one who'll go crazy. She'll have a fit. Then Paul and I—or somebody—will have to pick up the pieces."

It came out quickly, more than I should have said so early in the day. I'd known Liz at U.V.A.—we all had—and being around her tended to make me impatient. She and Mitch had fought a lot when they were dating, and he'd call me up, or Paul would, and I'd go to the boys' apartment for a bullshit session and beer. Mitch had been pretty frank in those days, and brittle. He'd pace and talk about how he didn't think every meal, every conversation, should be a test. How everyday love shouldn't be so hard. I wasn't living with Brian yet, but we were dating and got along well, systematically. I didn't have much sympathy for Mitch. If he wanted a less demanding girlfriend, I told him, he should change girlfriends. Instead, it seemed that Liz had changed Mitch and he'd allowed it to happen. Even now I sometimes found it hard to forgive him for no longer being smiling and safe, my little brother unadorned.

The look he gave me was close-mouthed, his blue eyes cloudy with the drift of polite vacancy. "Yeah, you're right. I'm being a softy. Let's take off." I felt a pang when he slapped the dog farewell on the slats of her rib cage.

I whipped the Jeep onto the highway, edging out a pickup filled with the jowly, disappointed faces of fishermen. The weather was frustrating everyone. I turned on the radio, caught static from WOBR, turned it off again.

"You know what I remember about the guy in Coinjock, the puppy man." Mitch looked out over the quartz light of the dunes as I spoke. His curls were shiny with sea salt. "His truck was full of sweet corn, some good, some wormy, and Mom was crazy about it, wanted two dozen ears or so. The dogs were an afterthought, just like the guy's kids. He had two dirty kids stuffed in the cab of that truck and about five yipping, dung-covered puppies. Remember that? It was hot as hell, and we were all grossed out by the smell except you and Mom. Your face was perfect when you saw those dogs. Like you were as happy as you'd ever be. Paul and I went into an instant sulk, we were so sure you'd get one. I don't know how Dad resisted."

"But he did." The sentence shot past my head.

"Yes," and I took my eyes off the road to say this, "because he was really into denying us things back then, they both were. Like we needed to respect how they were children of the Depression or something. God, I can remember those stupid, achy disappointments like not getting the exact goose-down jacket I wanted for Christmas. Do you ever think about things like that?"

Mitch rapped on the window glass with his knuckles. "Oh sure, everybody hates what they can remember."

"One of the kids in that truck was wearing torn red shorts and that's all. Nothing else. It had this scraggly hair and none of us could tell if it was a boy or a girl." Mitch kept tapping at the glass. I geared down and swung into the sandy entrance to Trent Drive. "You said you cried. That, I don't remember. I don't see you crying."

"Maybe I didn't," he said. "Maybe that never happened."

I shouldn't have been surprised when Mitch got out of the Jeep and went straight up the stairs to the roof deck, but I was. He'd always been the easygoing kid, the one impossible to bridle with seriousness. The abrupt silences and edgy brooding I'd seen that week reminded me of myself. I wondered if moodiness came with age for some people. Or maybe Mitch was more like me than I realized, had always been that way, and I was just hung up on our differences. I'd been big on categories as a child: Mitch was good with people, Paul was good at sports, I was good at organizing myself and everybody else.

The roof deck wasn't much more than a modified widow's walk, but you could see the ocean and Pamlico Sound from there, three hundred and sixty degrees of moon-drawn water. There was only one chair to sit in. Mitch had carried the other one downstairs the day we arrived at the cottage and no one had bothered to carry it back up. I took the groceries into the kitchen, wondering what to do while my brother paced the boards above me like a troubled, but still embodied, ghost.

I decided to set myself up on the screened porch with the bag of potato chips and a paperback biography Brian had given me when gifts were still easy. I'd let the wind and rain blow through, see what happened. I knew I'd regret it if Mitch didn't come down and talk to me, even if we only talked about baby Cece, or politics, or our mother's inexhaustible hostess cheer. I'd been a meandering failure recently—at love, and at the firm where the managing partner was breathing down my neck—and I wanted to tell some of this to Mitch. He'd been my best friend once, in his bursting, erratic way, and I wanted him to know I wasn't as standoffish as I'd been in college and law school. I'd changed, too. No matter what Brian thought, I *had* learned to buckle. And because we'd known each other before knowledge became the weight of our lives, I wanted to hear what my brother thought about the way cornered hearts gave in.

I was so absorbed in my book the bird flew right over me before I noticed it. I thought it was a bat at first—it was that frantic and quick. But when it hurled itself against an upper corner of the screen, I saw it was only a bird and a small one at that. Every movement I made provoked a furious flutter of wings, the hissing scrape of feathers against metal mesh. So I froze. I'd never been good with animals, especially the cats or horses or cockatiels that demanded a soothing, wise attention to their nerves. I was sure I'd make the bird hurt itself. So I decided to do what was easy—open the door to the outside and leave the rest to fate.

It didn't work. The bird was determined to exit the way it had entered, through a small gap near the ceiling, which I could see when I leaned to my left. When I noticed Paul's beach towel drying on a redwood bench, it occurred to me that I could use it like a net, capture the bird, then carry it onto the deck and release it into the sky. If I stayed calm, the story I'd have to tell Mitch and the family would have a sweet and careful end.

As soon as I grabbed up the towel, the bird was gone. It found its unshadowed seam and vanished. Relieved, my feet shuffling their way into an impromptu dance, I went to the kitchen for a tall glass of lemonade and ice. I hadn't heard a sound from the roof deck so I was sure Mitch was asleep, or petrified in some sort of protective gloom. I had to keep myself from going to him, from interrupting his chosen solitude. When I came back to the porch, I was able to single out the grating call of a boat-tailed grackle—one of the common island birds Mom had identified for me. The grackle was perched somewhere among the junipers along the path to the ocean; it sounded hoarse but confident, unfazed by the drizzle from the sky. I found myself hoping the weather would improve so Mitch and I could take a walk along the beach. I wanted to face him without a backdrop, ask him what was bothering him. We had always operated better in the open, I thought, where the vastness of the world caused us to draw close like cubs raised together in a dark, cramped den.

I fell asleep, the crash of the surf eroding to a calm lilt in my ears. The next thing I knew I was flat on my back, my chair collapsed beneath me, lemonade soaking my shirt. I knew what had happened even before I saw Mitch crouched in front of the picnic table. He was doubled over with laughter.

"Don't act so smart," I coughed. "That was totally unfair." I flung the soggy paperback past his head.

"You let your guard down, Annie. And you should never, ever do that with me or Paul around. Not even when you're ninety years old."

I scrambled to my feet and shifted my weight onto my toes, pure reflex. In one impetuous moment Mitch had flipped the pages back to the oldest, crudest rules—getting even, staying even. "When I'm ninety, asshole, you'll be in your rich doctor's grave."

"Maybe." He laughed even harder. "But you'll still be catching up."

For Mitch, teasing me was like performing a familiar card trick. He'd always been able to conjure up my temper; it was his ace, his margin of control. But his face went blank when I lowered my center of gravity and charged. My head, still light from my nap, felt strangely clear, and I realized our angers were no longer familiar to us, that this sudden clamor was like an unintelligible warning we were both shouting at the same time. Still, I squared Mitch in my sights, thinking *no holds barred.*

He dodged at the last second. His shoulder met the shallow cup of my hipbone, and I found myself in the high, white spiral of an airplane spin.

"You jerk," I shouted as he locked my legs against his chest. "Damn it, put me down."

And he did, after four or five giddy revolutions. My heart was pounding, my face flushed with blood that poured into all the wrong channels. I could smell it now—the sweat and bared flesh and torn grass of so many battles, ones I had been tearfully desperate to win. Heat. Pain. Childhood, savage and pure. Mitch rocked in front of me, breathing hard, his smile raw and devilish. He felt it, too. I could see that. Touching each other had brought something back. "I have to sit down," I said, reeling. "What about a beer?"

He brought two opened bottles from the kitchen, and we collapsed onto the sandy carpet. All right, I thought to myself, I've made my point. We don't have to say a single meaningful word until the others come back. We both know we're still panting and real.

"You deserved that," Mitch said, leaning back on his elbows. "More than anyone in the whole damn family."

I joshed along with him. "Oh, do docs always pound on their helpless sisters?"

He dropped his chin and shook his head as if there were water in his ears, then looked straight at me. "You're about as helpless as a shark. When you don't like something—like you don't like Liz, or Dad's political opinions—you take your toll. Don't think I've missed all the jabs."

I blinked, caught off guard again. "I never said I didn't like Liz."

"Not for four or five years, maybe, but I know how you feel. Paul, too. You guys are tough on her. You've never been on her side."

The muscles in my neck and jaw went hard. "That's not how it works, Mitch. I think you know that. We're on *your* side. Always."

"Yeah, well." He made a blotchy fist and ground it into the top of his thigh. "She's been talking about a divorce."

I'd known that somehow. Everyone in the family had. But we'd kept our thoughts to ourselves, maybe because of my niece Cece and the way she seemed to belong to us all.

"I'm sorry. You haven't looked very happy."

"What do *you* know about that?" The words were like rapid punches at my face. "I *am* happy. I know how I want to be. I've worked damn hard at it. But everybody wants a different piece of me, so I can't be some cheery little kid you remember, okay? You need to lay off."

Mitch's voice had gone high. Mine was stuck in my throat. I thought again of the grief he had shackled to his early love for his wife. He was so unshielded in some ways, so easily bruised. And I hadn't protected him at all.

"All right," I croaked. "I'll stay out of it."

"That would help."

I drew my knees to my chin and wished to hell our fishing trip hadn't been canceled, that we were still out there on the rough hem of the Atlantic, casting and reeling above the wordless deep. I thought about how I could be fairer to Liz, more giving, perhaps just more invisible.

How I could hope things worked out for them. I figured I could withstand the fact that Mitch hadn't even mentioned Brian's name, or given hard attention to my life. What I couldn't quite accept was that he didn't seem to want anything from me, not even simple generosity.

"Hey, Annie," he whispered, "do you see that?"

Feeling drained, I didn't answer. I saw him ease to his feet, one hand lifted above his head, his face as bright as if he'd just emerged from beneath a crashing wave. It was as though the subject of our intermingled lives was suddenly behind us, or had never been the subject of discussion at all. Mitch had left me. I felt the valves of my heart constrict as my blood slowed, preparing for the careful swerve into pleasantry that follows acknowledgment. Or near acknowledgment. For what had Mitch and I really told each other? Our words had been mostly awkward and blunt. Had we felt more than we'd said, agreed on something essential somewhere in the canals of nerve we shared? I wasn't sure. I only knew that I grieved for a moment passed, a dozen moments passing, and he did not.

I rubbed my eyes and looked at him again. The bird had returned, perched on a rolled-up window blind. Its feathers seemed somehow both green and yellow now as they caught a glint of the hanging sun. Mitch approached it, light chirps coming from his mouth. How did he do it? How did my disheartened brother know those ways of the world? In no time the bird hopped onto the white ledge of his forefinger and waited expectantly for the next crisp fragment of song. Mitch stood still then, but I could see how his body thrilled to its task. The loose folds of his cotton clothes seemed to shimmer.

Moments later, he eased toward the door, cautioning me with the darkened slant of his eyes not to move an inch. We also shared a brief smile fired by the kind of unburdened joy I thought he'd forgotten. Such courage, such trust—he seemed to say—all in a creature less substantial than a fringe of rag. Yet it was complex enough, our bird was; complicated enough for survival. My brother opened the screen door with the flat of his free hand, and the bird flew, a whir of meadow-fresh color against the fading scrim of poor weather. It landed on the eastern rail of the deck, a hard breeze combing its feathers, hopped once to assure itself of direction, and flew again.

Search Bay

At night the wind sometimes woke him as it sliced across the tin roof of the cabin, and he would open his eyes in darkness to find his hands gripping the bed frame. Thirty-five knots, forty knots—it was impossible not to gauge the speed of the gusts in his mind. He felt, too, the chastened shudder of a hull and the inevitable way his bones prepared themselves for a hard roll to port. The lake was a quarter-mile away, beyond two ridges feathered with birch and spruce, yet he could hear her, feel her. The wind might eventually shift to the south, or it might blow itself out. Still, he never again found sleep on those nights—a cruel, honest fact of his body. He lay alert on his thin mattress, boots and slicker hanging so close he could smell them, completing his watch as he must.

November. A month of change, a time of vigil. The last of the leaves flared and fell away, scouring the withdrawn horizon. Winter almost always broke over the bay like a green sea this time of year, this far north. It happened quickly, without much warning even to him, and he'd lived on this stretch of the Lake Huron coast all his life except when he'd been on the lakes, or tramping the Atlantic. He cut wood. He laid in kerosene and dry goods, reorganized supplies on the shelves of the cold porch until they made sense only to him. He repaired the roof, suffered a bitter night's rain, repaired the roof again. He visited his sister in town, took her a face cord of mixed hardwood even though she hadn't asked for it. He turned back the deer hunters who wandered east from the state forest. He studied the patterns of the crews from the power company as they did their last work of the year in his territory. It was a season of reckoning and recognition, one he liked to mull over. He was old. Preparation was the only rule left to live by.

On most days he walked down to the shore. It was the one aimless routine he allowed himself, and it was far better, he thought, than being part of the union flotsam that washed up on waves of coffee or worse, along the gangways of the Soo locks. Those were the men who couldn't break their habits, or didn't know they had them to begin with. Not that he avoided every laker he ran into. He did not. He'd taken his nephews to the locks once or twice, shared some stories with the jaw gang there. And he saw the old pissers in the Indian casinos when he went, former oilers and bosuns and mates exchanging their pension cash for lightweight tokens, their dark deck clothes replaced with golf shirts that made no sense on their bodies. He had little need for their sort of commerce. It was enough to come to the edge of the bay. Sniff at the nearly odorless water, utter the old names that gave character to its waves and the ranging grays of its skies. Mackinac, the queen island, stood some miles offshore, her bluffs a charcoal slash of shadow and spume. Often there would be a ship clearing the straits as well, and he would eye her as carefully as he dared, knowing there was a good chance he'd recognize her, that she'd been plying her trade when he'd been scrambling at his. Seven hundred feet long, a thousand feet long, riding high on ballast or filled with grain, phosphates, maybe ore. There was a great deal he could tell from a glance. Yet all he really found himself studying was her silhouette and her motion, knowing she held desperate men. November, and the ice was not here yet, the gales were still howling their chorus to the north. A walk to the rocky, wind-whisked shore of the bay. A savored cigarette. The rest of the day for the simpler, bracing tasks he now asked of himself.

He had the bulldozer out of the shed the day the boy came. He was lubing the blade lifts and half-tinkering with the engine, which was how he explained his unreadiness when it needed to be explained. There was a locked gate between his place and the state road two miles west. No one was supposed to bother him except the Sandhursts, who used his track to get to their cottage, and maybe the Mahans, who owned a few acres along the shore to the southeast. Even his brother Otto didn't come out here. Too far from town, Otto said. They could talk at the shop if they needed to talk, or at their sister's. Then the boy appeared, on foot, moving like he knew where he was going and why. He was startled and felt surprise flutter across his face like a dusky wing just before he went spiteful.

If the boy said hello, he never heard it. But the boy did stop walking, waiting for a moment on the wet leaves of the path, which allowed him to cut the grind of the bull-dozer's diesel to silence. It was as though the afternoon went dead when he did that—no noise, no heat or vital stink from the engine. The boy was dressed in a red-plaid wool coat, jeans, a beaten felt hat, no gloves. He looked warm enough though he wasn't wearing any blaze orange, which made him a damn fool. Dark eyes and skin, flattish nose, wide jaw. Chippewa, maybe, though it wasn't a face he recognized. If the boy was poaching, he'd gotten half smart and stashed his gun. If he was just wandering, he'd made a considerable mistake.

He laid his crescent wrench in the toolbox bolted be-hind the seat of the dozer. It was the boy's place to get nervous and speak.

"Came for the beaver." The voice was quick and ca-sual, though deep enough to make him believe the boy was older than he looked.

"Don't look like you came ready for much of any-thing." He waved at the boy's empty hands and began a controlled laugh, wondering if the boy had heard any bad stories about him and the lonely way he lived in the woods. He hoped he had. "You shouldn't be here."

"I got the permission." The boy swung an arm down the track past the cabin. "Man called from Lansing, having trouble with too many beaver."

He understood then, enough of it. A portion of Sandhurst's land had been flooded all spring and summer; they'd had a helluva time with the road. He'd been over there a time or two himself to clear the dammed culverts. Once he'd spent part of a morning taking potshots at the animals as they swam across their new pond, but he hadn't hit anything. Beaver learned fast. He'd told Sandhurst he'd trap them out if he wanted. Sandhurst, it looked like, had decided to do it right. Indians had unrestricted rights to trap beaver The boy was definitely Indian.

"You know what you're doing, go on."

"I know what I'm doing." The boy shrugged his wrists up into the sleeves of his plaid coat. "My uncle said to come out here and look it over. He also said to come to you, let you know. His legs are bad today."

"You walk in from the gate?"

The boy nodded.

"Sandhurst plan to send you a key?"

A shrug again like that didn't really matter. The boy lifted one foot, then the other, restless. The boots he wore were too large for him and cracked along the soles. They'd be wet and awkward in the bogs.

"Who's your uncle? He know me from somewhere?"

The boy stepped back like he'd been cut loose by the question. "He didn't say to talk about it." A straight look, black-eyed. "Just said to tell you I had the job. If you knew that, he said, I'd be all right."

It made his chest burn in the old way to watch the boy walk off like he did, easy, preoccupied. He'd be a better man, he thought, if he didn't want to bust everybody like they were on his crew. Yet it was the truth that he sometimes lost his taste for people for weeks at a time. It always came back to him, a doglike understanding of companionship. But as warm and viscous as the feeling was on its return, this desire to tolerate others, to congregate with them, it remained fickle within him. It made him a disappointment, too—he knew that—but he hadn't decided to live any other way.

The boy's face came back to him when the day was done. He hadn't left by the road, choosing to hack through the undergrowth instead, or to follow the rocky hip of the lake. That was how he imagined it anyway—the boy's evasion. But as he fried his potatoes and onions in a skillet, the broad face with the angled, assessing eyes came back to him. The boy reminded him a little of Henderson, that was the only connection he could make. Henderson was an Indian, too, from somewhere up in New York State, and he'd been a cook on the *Pontiac* for a while. Reasonable cook, reasonable man. Not much remarkable about him, though he never ran short of coffee, ever, which was a good trait in a galley man. Most of his people walked steel in Pittsburgh or New York City, that's what he said, but he'd signed onto a freighter out of Buffalo after his stint in the army and never looked back. Henderson told some good stories, as most cooks did—he remembered that. The man kept his hair braided, he told stories while he worked both messes, officers' and crew's, he stayed out of people's business. It was funny he even recalled Henderson; he'd worked with hundreds of men on a long line of ships. But this was the *Pontiac,* old and cranky even when he hadn't been, running coal up the dark spine of Lake Erie, her every inch, he remembered, stinking of black dust and hurry. Henderson had never been able to cook a meal that didn't taste of it.

Later, when he was on his bunk with the radio turned low, a hockey game from endless Canada, he believed Henderson hadn't been on the *Pontiac* at all. It had been the bad luck *McCurdy.* Memories lagged and heeled, and he understood he'd hoped to fool himself. Yet even as he closed his eyes he found he could clarify little more than the smell of burnt anthracite and onion. Henderson would have laughed to hear it. No ship's cook he knew had ever been so bad he ruined onions.

He turned off the radio and lay square on the bunk. It seemed as though he ought to prepare himself for something that was as yet out of sight, beyond guessing. The thing he called his storm sense was tracking a disturbance; he felt the fine tingle in his skull. A low-pressure system, maybe. Illness. Maybe ghosts. He'd have to bide his time before he knew.

The snow came. Not enough to plow but enough to blanket the ground, quilt its mineral smells, leave him to feel like his season had begun. Most of the years he'd sailed on the lakes they'd made it into December, the ice of Superior would hold off that long, so he wasn't home to see the tatted crystals begin to fringe the bay or to taste the air's last flavor of earth. He returned to a world already insulated and hard. There were the years he'd bunked in Toledo, of course. Not so cold there, or easy. That was when he'd been married, had a house, aimed to study his way off deck and onto the bridge, a foolishness he'd undertaken for Mary and her sad, pleading face, though it had been a good thing in the end. Officers served two months on, two off. Able-bodied seamen worked as many voyages as they could hustle. Mary believed she wanted him home in that gum-green cottage above the scudding Maumee. So he studied when he could and parlayed his long years aboard into favors. Made himself into a third mate from nothing in the days when such a thing could still be done. Then he lost Mary.

He gathered half a sack of Idas from the cold porch and set off down the track, his head soon clear in the still, dry air. He took the apples up on a knoll he knew, one that had the black trickle of a spring at its base. The deer would find the shriveled fruit by sundown. He fed them most of the winter if he could—carrots, apples, acorns—not so he could hunt them, but so he could know they were there and that they would stay there, in his woods, because of him. He hadn't taken a buck on his own property in several years. Foolishness, no doubt, but it was a foolishness he could afford. His family had owned this land above the bay for more than a hundred years. They'd logged it, fished it, trapped it, hunted it, tried to sell it to rich people from downstate who didn't stick. Now they held it because it was easy to hold and righteous to claim. He stayed there because his brother and sister didn't care if he did otherwise, and because it was good for him to be planted, safer. It made him pay attention to himself—this place that expected little of him, which needed even less than he gave. The lakes had not been like that.

He'd nearly ruined the memory because he'd dragged it out so much, the one about how he got his start on water. He'd been young and crazy and skittish, enraged by his father in all the usual ways. So he hitched rides on mail boats and farm trucks, made his way to Leland where there was damn near nothing to do, and lied himself onto a leaky, jury-rigged vessel named the *Alma L.* They wanted him on the black gang shoveling coal, but when he convinced them he halfway knew how to navigate and that he'd skidded his share of logs in his life, they put him on the deck crew instead. It was merciless work, yet he loved it in ways it took him years to understand.

Weather and exasperation, water and breakdown—he went at it all.

The captain was an arrogant drunk who used his instruments and charts when he felt like it. The mate, soon satisfied that he couldn't buffalo the new boy, gave him half of his own job to do, and he lasted at it as long as the *Alma L.* did. The captain ran her across a bar near the Manitous in a spunky summer storm; the mean pounding they took there snapped the chain to her rudder. Another vessel answered the captain's obscene distress call and was able to put a line across *Alma*'s bow, but it was clear they'd need to jettison cargo if they hoped to be pulled free. The old man went into a blind rage when he heard that, calling for barges to take on his pulpwood, then for a breeches buoy rescue, though they were too far from shore for that, and no one but the captain himself was old enough to have ever seen such a thing. He helped the mate cut loose a level of logs, but the captain ordered them to stop and struck them both across the face with a leather lanyard. It was the first act of shipboard madness he'd seen.

Since they weren't allowed to rebalance her load, the *Alma L.* listed starboard and eventually heeled over in the waves. He later heard that she was salvaged and that she and her captain made hell and money in those waters for many years after. He, however, disappeared as quietly as he'd come, heading south until he found deck passage across Lake Michigan to Wisconsin. He'd been told that the place he needed to be was Duluth.

Freighters reigned over both the Iron Range and the big waters up there. He left for a few unsatisfactory tries at the Atlantic and a stint in the merchant marine during the war, but he was never on salt water for long. There was a belief within him, even at sixteen, that some men were meant to labor their way toward extremes of their own choosing.

He walked until he couldn't think about that version of himself anymore, then he turned back. He skirted the thicket of the cedar bog, passed close to a bear's den he knew about, eyed the empty trees. On his way to the cabin he saw a speckled scatter of feathers near the splintered stump of a pine and realized that there was a thing he would miss until spring, the shy occupation of the loons on the bay, the full sound of their inhuman laughter.

Some days later the boy left him a note on the ground near his door. *Set 3 traps,* it said. *Uncle still sick.* The note was written in pencil on a large, silvery square of birch bark. Its letters were careful and upright. The boy had even signed his name. Frank Andrews. When he walked out to the track he could see the muddy, bowlegged wells made by the boy's misfit boots as he labored under the weight of his traps. A stagger coming and going, and that was all.

That night he awoke in his chair near the stove only to realize that his deck crew had not run short of paint and primer, that his boiling anxiety about a young wheelman was phantom vapor and heat. He thought about taking a drink. He thought about going beyond solitude toward something dark and squatting entirely. He believed he'd been talking in his sleep, though to whom he couldn't say.

His sister Frieda liked him to come for Sunday dinner, so he went when he felt like it or guessed she could use a little money or help around the house. Cecil, her husband, was a long-haul trucker who did what he could when he had the time. Frieda had been talking for years now about how good things would be when Cecil finally got a job at the prison. But prison jobs were hard to come by; they paid damn well. People waited a long time.

Frieda never said much about the money he slipped her when he visited. He told her to consider it rent since he was living on property that belonged to all three of them. She kept the books for a gift shop in town and made a few things to sell there herself—wood-burnt plaques and Snow Island table runners—but she mostly stayed home with the boys. She'd take the money from him, her big brother, and thank him for something else, firewood or a door he'd rehung. They both knew if they stooped to talking about money, they'd end up discussing the years he'd traded most of his for liquor.

This Sunday they had sauerbraten that Frieda had marinated, and mashed potatoes, and a salad thrown together by the boys. He was in the kitchen smoking the one cigarette his sister allowed; his nephews were watching football on the TV in the den. Somehow it came about that he told Frieda of the boy's visit to the beaver ponds. Nothing else had happened to him in the last few weeks unless he counted finding a gutshot doe near the north edge of the bog a piece of news, and Frieda didn't like to hear about things like that. Ravens had led him to the doe, the heavy way they croaked and gathered in the treetops attracting his attention more than usual, and he'd cut the doe's throat with his knife though she was nearly dead anyway. Frieda wouldn't want to hear about the ravens either, or the raucous bald eagles, or the chipmunk that desperately wanted to hibernate on his porch. His sister like to hear about the human leftovers, snapped saw blades or rusted drag chains, implements that proved the Hansens had broken their backs and spilled their sweat out there in the woods like any other family with an honest history. She also liked him to talk about how things were along the western shallows of the bay where they'd built tepees of birch saplings and bark when they were children, the three of them, and their father took them camping. She loved that place, she said, how the yellow sun fell off behind the spiked fence of the pines, the way grilling fish smelled, and she would never forget it. She wished Cecil would take the boys there, just pitch a tent and forget about the motorboat for one damn day. But she never suggested he take his nephews instead, as though it would not be the right favor to ask, as though his choice to live the way he did now, just like his choice to sign onto a steamer thirty-some years before, was the wrong combination of impulsiveness and love.

"You say his name is Andrews?" Frieda scraped hard at a crusted pot. "Paula Andrews's got a son still in school and I know you know Paula."

Frieda didn't bother to turn away from the sink after she spoke, but he understood he was about to be punished. "Chad," she shouted, "get your butt in here."

There were groans and the padded sounds of a scuffle before his oldest nephew appeared in the doorway with his forearms folded across his black T-shirt. He felt Chad look at him neutrally, the one house guest he didn't have to behave for. They'd had a short conversation at dinner about his Venezuelan tattoo and how much it had hurt, and they'd talked about the Lake State hockey team. It had been enough for both of them.

"Frank Andrews go to school with you?"

"Not no more. Dropped out." Chad lifted his arms above his head and mimed a jump shot. "Chip kid. You know how it is."

"I know it's tough for everybody." Frieda dried her palms on her skirt, looked at him, then away. "Take the garbage out, will you, then go on back and behave. Leave your brother alone."

Chad headed toward where his boots were sprawled on a rug by the door. "His mom's the one works at the bar."

"I know that," Frieda snapped. "I better not find out you've been over there."

Chad clomped out the door without his coat, and his

sister turned on him. “Get what you came for, Johnny? I could have hooked you up with Paula without feeding you a good dinner.”

He spun his glazed coffee mug between his hands. There were lots of Andrewses between here and the Soo. He hadn’t really thought about the boy belonging to Paula. “I haven’t been in there in a long time,” he said. “Not since before I retired.”

Frieda sat opposite him at the table. Her fair skin was smooth and pretty, flushed with the anger she’d stirred up, but still pretty. He was more than ten years older than she was, and there’d been times he’d taken care of her as well as any parent could. “I guess I’d be the first to hear otherwise since the place is still packed with tattlers and assholes. I’d like to keep Chad out of there. He takes after Cecil’s side, too slow to stay out of trouble. Not like his uncle.”

He listened to her voice, careful and parched with forgiveness. Cecil ought to be around more, he thought, or somebody should. “Paula Andrews just poured the drinks I ordered,” he said. “And it’s all over anyhow. I don’t have time to drink.”

Frieda laughed then, raising her chin and flexing her shoulders just as their father had when things were right with him. “You got time to do nothing *but* drink, so you give it up like a stubborn bastard. John Hansen, always cutting his own trail.”

He stood, the trill of her chuckle running through him. Frieda closed things up between them; she always had. She flattened her hand as he slipped a fifty-dollar bill from his pocket. "Take the leftovers with you, do that much," she said. "And thank you for the wood. Chad and C.J. stacked it like you taught them. It's worked out good."

He drove as if he were in a hurry until he reached the blinking yellow light across from the grocery where he turned toward the water. He drifted past the house of a childhood friend who was on disability from his job with the road commission. Two doors down was the brown, asbestos-shingled bungalow his own family had lived in during a good stretch. The lake was in front of him, broken up by the gaunt reach of a few docks and the frosted cluster of Les Cheneaux Islands. The water here looked black, but common, polished into a series of pathways that led from shelter to shelter.

He parked, but it wasn't until he was out of the truck, his fingers working at the large horn buttons of his jacket, that he realized he was just up the block from the Chinook. He'd been thinking about Otto and how he was going to drop by the shop to say hello. His fidgeting had driven everything else from his head. Everything except muscle memory. He walked across the damp, deserted street and looked in the storefront window of the bar. Closed until four. Chairs upended on the tables like spindly carcasses. Pool table in the same naked place. There were plastic garlands strung with Christmas lights nailed inside the window frame, though the lights weren't plugged in, and he could see a pall of fine dust on the sprigs of false holly and cedar. There was a tiny crèche nestled in cotton wadding on the varnished windowsill as well. Touches of Paula. Sweet. Well-meaning. Incomplete. He reopened the top button of his coat and began to search for his gloves. He'd lived a piece of his life in the Chinook, fighting, paring down love, filling his core with the false heat of bourbon. Then he'd moved on. The building felt no different in his mind now than the small dog-brown bungalow hunkered just out of sight on this same hill. He would swear to that.

He knew Otto would be working, even with the marina shut until spring, because that's what Otto did. His brother had repainted the building that fall, and he'd put in double-paned windows and new barn red awnings. But he hadn't changed the name of their father's business. It was the same. *Hansen and Sons. Boatbuilders. Docks. Storage.*

He knocked on the bolted front door, though he had a key to the lock on his own key ring. Otto had never been one for surprises. He waited, then heard a motor fire up just as he was setting his face to meet his brother's. The engine sounded muted and sluggish in the cold. He stepped around the corner of the shop, across the old launch ramp that was now boarded up, and toward the quay. His brother was casting off in the Chris-Craft, his face a putty-colored mask above his coveralls and the thick, speckled scarf done up for him by his wife, Marge. The gunwales and windshield of the boat were glazed with ice, and the inlet was curdled with slush. Boxes and bags crowded the floor of the boat behind where Otto stood at the wheel, his movements stiff but sure as he throttled into the channel. He was running groceries to widows and shut-ins living on the islands, stern and charitable with his yellow Labrador braced against his legs, her nose raised in the slapping air. That was his younger brother, as able and Lutheran as they came. He watched Otto take the chill breath of the lake across his face, watched him handle himself as any good wheelman might as his wake spooled and crimped the dark water. Something about the sight made his neck feel bowstrung, but he conquered it. Then he worked his way back to his still warm truck and the narrow, patchy roads to the bay.

The boy came when the girl got hurt, and it later seemed to him that the boy, Frank Andrews, had guessed they'd be shut up in a room together one day, that he was somehow prepared for it. He was patching the wall behind his woodstove with metal cut from a wrecked panel truck because it's what he had for the job. There'd been a wet five-inch snow the night before; he didn't feel like plowing his way toward town. Besides, he liked an ugly repair that called on him to be resourceful.

The cabin door was open a crack for fresh air, but the boy knocked on the jamb anyway. The noise of the knock pivoted him against the stove, crouching. Then he saw it was the boy from the brownish slash of face, the drained color of his hat. "Yeah." He stood with the hammer still in his hand.

"It's Frank Andrews." The boy laid out each syllable like it was stolen. "Got my beaver, but had a accident with a trap and wondered if you had a bandage. Just till I can get to my car."

He went to the door with purpose then, knowing that cold and shock could make a bad thing seem not so bad at first. A man could break an arm in one of those traps. The snow spitting from the low, marbled sky had begun to dust the boy's sturdy shoulders with flakes. He took in the boy's eyes, which were black and even and undeluded by pain, then he saw the sleek carcass of a beaver cast into a pocket drift near a corner of the shack. It was bloodless as it ought to be since the traps were made to drown a beaver and never tear its pelt. It took him a moment to register the girl standing half-shielded by the boy. She was the one who'd been hurt. One of her hands was cupped beneath the other like a bowl, collecting the run of blood.

"Get in here," he said, "get on in," and he didn't take time to say what he wanted to say about the cramped way he lived. The blood he'd seen was bright red, but there wasn't much of it. There'd be more in the heat of the cabin, but if she hadn't nicked an artery he supposed he could handle it. Otherwise, it would be compresses and blankets and a damn crazy dozer ride out to the road. Neither kid did anything more than cross the threshold, but the boy reached for the girl's elbow as if to offer her rivuleted skin as evidence of some sort of sincerity. "I got a first-aid kit," he said before either of them could start with an explanation. "Sit her in my chair and lay that hand where I can see it."

Coat and cap off, hands washed, kit opened on the table, which was scoured smooth and clean because he kept it that way. He'd never served as purser onboard, but he'd cleaned up his share of sailors after fights or mishaps with winches and snapped lines. He'd doctored himself plenty, too. He placed a towel under the girl's blood-mapped wrist. Her eyes were a shiny tannin brown, contracted some with pain and worry, though her cold-flushed mouth flitted with a smile that was part embarrassment, part apology. Indian, too, he decided, though not as full-blooded as the boy. Her hair was pulled off her face and hung down her back in a smooth, water-beaded hank. It was easy for him to see that she was pretty. Of course, any son of Paula's would be used to that, fine looks in a woman, though whether he'd come to expect it, to search for it, was maybe another matter. He laid his own toughened fingertips at the base of her hand, felt it quiver, yet coaxed her without words to open her fingers. She shivered all over then, and he remembered what little he'd seen of her when she'd been standing on his doorstep. She was wet to the waist, soaking wet, as anybody might be who went after beaver dressed in jeans and cheap stay-in-town boots. He nodded to the boy, who was hovering at the edge of the table. "Build up the fire, will you? Or the hypothermia will get to her before I do."

The cut was ragged and ran from the crease of her ring finger across her palm to the fleshy base of her thumb, which accounted for the good amount of blood. Her thawing hands ached and stung; he could see that, too. And before he thought about it he was massaging them with his own, his skin feeling husklike to him against the raw damp of hers. She was small-boned, trembling. He daubed at her palm with a corner of the towel, then looked into her eyes, which gave him nothing. Without wiping his own fingers clean, he began to irrigate the wound.

"I can fix this good enough to get you to the clinic. You going up to the Soo?"

Neither of them answered him at first, though the girl dropped her head so he could see its delicate oval crown, the pale scar of her part.

"St. Ignace," the boy said from where he was squatting by the stove. "She's from there."

"They got a Indian clinic there, somewhere she can get stitches?"

"It'll get taken care of." The boy's voice was harder than it needed to be, and he wondered if they'd both been scared out there, truly afraid they were up against it, and that was what was holding them in so tight. Then again, maybe he'd made some kind of mistake. Maybe the girl wasn't Indian at all.

"Good," he said. "You take care of it. Because I can sew it up here and now if you're planning on getting stupid on me, or lazy."

The girl flinched so hard her knuckles knocked against the tabletop. The boy, Frank, stood halfway and took on a look that read mad-as-hell, that made him feel solid to see, because he knew how to deal with an angry man, whereas this other, this unprepared for ministering, had brought a floating feeling to his stomach that he did not care for.

"Don't do no more." The boy moved up against the table again. "She's all right. Shelley, you all right?"

She nodded and began to push away from the heavy oak table, her hand stained orange with disinfectant but unbandaged, gaping. She seemed caught in the swift stream of the boy's assurance. Her legs failed her, though, faster than even he'd foreseen, because they'd been half-assed, all of them, and hadn't stripped her of her wet boots and clothes. She sank toward the chair, faltered, fell against the boy. He caught her under the arms and lifted her as though he'd cradled her before, then carried her to the bunk without asking. That was fine though, he thought. It was the right thing to do.

"We need to get her dry," he said to the boy, aware that his voice had gone solemn and whispery, though the girl was very much awake. "I got some clothes. See if she'll undress." He went to the place he kept his chest and flipped open the smooth brass latches while they spoke in low voices behind him. Everything in the chest was neatly folded and held the warm, powdery scent of cedar. It was easy to find what he needed.

"She wants to dress herself," the boy said, and the

girl who was sitting upright now on his scarred bunk, swung her head in blank agreement. "You . . . we . . . ," the boy half-coughed, "we make her nervous. Could we leave for a minute, let her take care of it?"

"Yes," he said, and that was all. He scooped up his cap and coat from the floor where they'd fallen and headed out the door. He'd forgotten to expect modesty from the young.

Frank Andrews closed the door behind them, and the clean, diffuse light the snow carried with it made it seem as though they'd stepped into a white, high-ceilinged room, one just large enough to handle their talk and commotion. He stepped over to the plump carcass of the beaver, knelt next to it. Its dead eyes and yellowed teeth were invisible, buried, yet he thought he could smell the oily, musky taint of panic.

"You planning to haul it out yourself?" The beaver was big, sixty pounds easy.

"She's strong," the boy said, tilting his head toward the cabin. "That's why I brung her along."

He laughed until the boy showed his well-spaced teeth, and then it was in him, fast and mean, to give his laugh an ugly twist. A girl like that shouldn't be out here, though he thought he understood why she'd come. The boy was rocking on his feet again, rippling with the unguided energy of a young man, an unbeaten one. Women would follow the stream of that energy as long as the boy had it, he thought. Follow it and try to drink it down.

Before he knew it, he'd reached into his pocket for two cigarettes and a lighter. It amazed him, the way two people could make headway without words. He thought briefly of the girl drying her small, cold-clenched body with his bath towel, the live tinge that would come to her skin, the darkening smears of her blood. Then something about the way the boy handled his cigarette, his whole body sheltering the lighter's blue-whipped flame, brought a question to mind. "You play some basketball?" He tapped his own smoke on a thumbnail. "I think my nephew talked about that."

The boy narrowed his eyes as if he were measuring something. He raised one hand, cocked it at the wrist, then flipped it forward. He could see that was all the answer he would get. It was over. The boy had left it behind. And even though his body remembered the moves, would forever remember them, he'd stopped tunneling into that game with his mind.

"We can stand out here and freeze then, just standing here. Or we can load that beaver in my truck." He bent over and scythed the snow off the glossy pelt with the edge of his hand. "I'll take you out to your car."

The boy squinted at him through a scrim of smoke, then shrugged the way he did.

"Check on her first, maybe," he said. "Make sure she's using the blankets."

The boy grabbed at his frosted hat and stuck his head back inside the cabin. He could see that the boy's hair had been cut since he'd last seen him. It fell in a smooth, blunt line along the flat muscle of his jaw and the coppery nape of his neck.

"She's all right," the boy said, fitting his hat back onto his head. "Dressing."

They squatted as a pair and shared the beaver's weight as they lifted. He glanced up the track and made a guess that the Ford would get to the road all right; it would be a lot easier if they could travel in a heated cab. When the beaver was laid out in the truck bed, he found his fingers spidering through his pockets for more cigarettes. The boy seemed impressed that he had two trucks in the shed, plus the dozer and a good canoe. He wanted to know about the machines, if they all drove well.

"Used to know your mother," he said to the boy instead, and right away the words hung from him like brittle ice from a branch. He felt foolish. The boy probably knew all he wanted to know about old Hermit Hansen. He had no business trying to make himself out to be another kind of man.

"Everybody knows my ma." The boy ran a hand along the searing green flank of the Ford, admiring the tires, the roomy bed. "Everybody from around here, anyway. Long time she's worked at the Chinook."

"I shot pool in there some, when I wasn't shipped out."

"Thought you hardly ever left this place." The boy blew some air into his hands, kept his eyes on the truck. "Guard it like a damn Doberman or something."

Hearing that strangled the bland words he'd aligned

in his throat, and he stepped out of the shed into a dervish of snow that whirled off the roof. He tried to lock his mind onto the idea of the half-dressed girl, how she needed to be wreathed in warmth, gotten home.

"Hey, you want to tell me about my ma, go ahead." There was swagger in the boy's words now. "I've heard it before. One million times. So don't think you know a story that'll get to me. You don't know a story like that."

He turned on the boy, headed back to where he stood in the shelter of the shed. But he couldn't get his head to go all silky like it needed to be before he went into a fight. He couldn't even bring Paula's smooth, silent, commiserating face into focus, her sympathetic neck. He stopped, letting the wind split at his back.

"I guess now you're gonna tell me Ma's the reason you keep women's clothes way out here." The boy had his arms away from his sides, hands flexing. "Do it then. Come at me with your weird-old-man shit. 'Cause no woman would ever come here for you. You can't tell me that."

It had been a long while since he'd been where the anger took him, riding roughshod through nerve and vein, howling within him louder than the words in his bitten throat could howl. Yet it came easily enough. He didn't bother to wait for the boy, who became like a broken-winged bird to him, clucking and fluttering in outrage. He went straight to the cabin, burst inside with his vision blanched by fury and the ungiving glare of snow. The girl was slumped on his bunk, drowsy maybe, wilted by comfort. He grabbed her where her shoulder met her collarbone, bent on flinging her to her feet, which he did. She gasped, and he felt her warm, shocked, caressing breath but didn't hear it. Didn't hear the boy tear into the cabin either, though he knew when he was behind him, exactly there, and was able to meet him with a solid punch to the gut when it was time. He flung the girl's short-waisted coat after her and her false-furred boots and her wet, crumpled clothes. He flung them both out, into the world where they could keep their messes to themselves. The girl began to cry, but he was deaf to that also. He did see the boy's face, though, and he knew what it meant, the black line of brows, the jagged, uncentered glint in the eyes. It meant the boy had been cornered for the first time. That he'd just about found a new edge to plunge over.

He barely heard the bleating curses and the crude battering of his truck as they tore at the tailgate and took their beaver back. They would have stolen the truck if they could have, maybe even wrecked it. It's what he would have done. He watched them hump up the track with the beaver bowing the boy's infuriated young body, the girl stumbling along behind. He noticed that the girl had left her soaked garments strewn between the cabin and the shed, and he thought he could either burn them or fold them into his sea chest—that it wouldn't matter which he did. He saw, too, that she'd wrapped her hand with the gauze he'd laid out for her. There was the blankness of a bandage on her, just as there was the resin color of corduroys on her legs, the noon-blue print of a turtleneck on her slender torso and arms, the musky linger of her sweat. What he didn't know and couldn't give a good history to were those vagabond clothes, what she'd taken from him. He did not recall who they'd once belonged to or whether he'd known her name at all.

The nights became as long as they ever get, and as stark, and the wave-etched ice shelved itself around the bay and out into the lake until the shipping channels were closed. Snow came in sheets and squalls and perfect geometric drifts. On clear days he hauled wood in the restless company of crows, skidding pallets of poplar and deadfall oak in from the far-off places he'd stacked them. On days when the sky seemed no higher than the treeline and the smoke from his chimney fumed at his door, he stayed in, flipped cards, listened to the insistent radio. He spent some complicated hours with a T square drawing up plans for a sauna, but he did not keep at it.

One night he pried open a carton of cigarettes and thought about the boy. He hadn't been back for his traps. It was no way to run a line, but laziness of that sort was up to the boy and his uncle, if there really was an uncle. He considered how he'd once connected the boy with Henderson and what a mistake that had been. Henderson had a sense of humor and a bolt-tight sense of himself as a man. Henderson had never thrown anything in another man's face, which was where the boy's weakness was, in his impetuous, assuming pride. Good sailors withheld almost all there was to withhold aboard ship—it was how any crew avoided murder—and if a sailor was smart, he behaved much the same way when he had to be on land. Surviving. Two legs to stand on.

Henderson on the *McCurdy.* They'd been aboard together, hauling a capacity load of taconite out of Duluth, running to make St. Marys River before she froze. On his first watch they took white water across the bow, and some of the vessels ahead—especially the empty ones—heaved to in the lee of Keweenaw Point or short of the river where thick fog was said to be mothering chunk ice and sleet. The *John C. McCurdy* steamed on. He had little trouble driving her into the black, foaming swells and keeping her trim. At next watch though, things were different.

The captain was on the bridge by then, sleepless, thin-lipped. The wind screeched through the gangways, and the water they took across the bow began to rivet itself into a crystal armor of ice. Radio reports put them on the near side of a full-blown gale. The captain was an able man, overly cautious but never stupid. He ordered a change of course designed to run with wind and current alike. But the *McCurdy* began to wallow under the extra weight of the ice. Two hours later the propeller gave way, unable to take the strain of being pitched into open air, then slammed into the mad roil of a twenty-foot crest. They all felt it, the wrench and give, and they hated the loss of momentum, the wheezing surge that had been the one force under their control. The captain radioed the Coast Guard and prepared for a merciless wait.

A twin-screw freighter from Canada offered to back-track and give the *McCurdy* a line to keep her off the shoals. But the captain told the freighter to tend to her own needs; he was nearly far enough east to be safe. And this was how Third Mate Hansen left things when he climbed from the bridge. Square-shouldered men not thinking ahead. Stoic.

He came into the officers' mess dripping and swearing. The air in the galley was stale with breath and sweat and the soggy smell of food no one wanted. He coughed into his hands, tasting the layered man-stink while he exhaled the arctic swipe of the storm. He noticed there was a passenger in the galley, a smallish withered man who was trying to read a magazine. It bothered him that the man was not in his cabin puking into his steel bowl and staying clear of a crew that had trouble on its hands, but he said nothing.

"Sandwich," he called to Henderson, and he shed his rain gear behind the chair that was his. Sloppy, irregular, but he did it anyway. The ship fell off into a trough; each man braced himself for dive and recovery. Devil's pride, he told himself, all of them pretending this cork-tossing was normal.

"I got some fish and some ham," Henderson said, his dark arms crossbarred in the doorway. "Your choice, sir."

That made them both laugh. "Make me four hams to run topside with some coffee. I can't stay here."

"Sure, you can. No man is that everlasting important." The words came from the passenger, sudden and taunting. He glanced at Henderson for confirmation of the man's impertinence, but Henderson had turned to his work, bowed and uninvolved, so he angled his body across the long, tilting table toward the stranger.

"Maybe I don't care if I'm important. It's my job."

"No, it's not, Mate Hansen. You've pulled your watch. You were off at twelve bells."

"This is a bad time, sir."

"This," the man said delightedly, "is what a freshwater sailor would call a bad time."

The old fellow, he decided, was crazy with worry, or simply crazy. He yanked his slicker from the floor while the *McCurdy* balanced atop yet another wind-shorn crest. He moved into the galley as she paused, looking for a place to steady himself because he didn't like the way she felt, bovine, resigned. The ship plunged hard, then submarined. He found himself pressed next to Henderson in the tight space below the ovens. The Indian showed clenched teeth. The passenger, it sounded like, was flung against a wall. Seconds later the bow pulled free of the water, and they were afloat again. They'd need worse luck to lose her—he knew that—but the captain would want him to ready the boats just the same.

Henderson went to help the passenger while he tucked his pockets full of sandwiches and a thermos. He listened as the passenger insisted he was unhurt. "I am fine," he chided the cook. "You men have been through nothing if you can't chin up to this." Henderson said something inaudible, and the passenger began to cackle, then cough. "I've been washed ashore bare-arsed twice in my life. You ever sail Torpedo Alley off Cape Hatteras? Ever hear of the bloody hell called Dunkirk?" He paused long enough to hear the man's hollow accent become more British than it had been before. The captain had passed along a name at one point—Burley? Billingsley?—a joyrider, the captain said, with plenty of money. He fastened his slicker and made his way to the corner where Henderson had propped the man upright.

"Ready to take to the boats, are you?" He leaned into the yellowish, translucent face that up close seemed shrunken by illness. He hadn't seen that before, or the blood dribbling from a split lip, and he felt pity mix with frustration in his gut, a blend he didn't like. "I ran the war blockade off Hatteras. Saw good ships go down. If that's what you're after, I'll make it my business to see you don't get it."

"You don't give the orders." The man bared his pinkened teeth for a laugh.

He grabbed the man's throat, sank his fingers into slack, wattled flesh, and shoved until the galley wall banged, then banged again. "I give the orders needed, you bastard. Go back where you came from and do it while you can."

He stood and wiped the spit from his lips. The *McCurdy* chose that moment to slither and spasm beneath them. He could sense the massive torque along her keel.

"There it is, Mate Hansen," the voice at his feet wheezed. "You feel it. You'll be my man before all's well and done."

He struck the man outright. With the flat of his hand at first, then his rapid fist. The old fellow closed his eyes and his head went loose on his neck as though he'd been beaten before and knew how to take it. Three punches, maybe four. He stopped when the cartilage of the thin, arrogant nose gave way beneath his knuckles.

It was Henderson who surprised him. The cook looked as if he planned to drive his own fist into the man's sunken gut. Yet he somehow fell away from the scarecrow collapse of the passenger, every glint of irritation and resolve drained from his eyes. His grim mouth moved in silence. He watched Henderson hard until the cook gasped as if he'd just discovered air. It was the ship, he thought. The damned strangling ship. Or the garrote of the storm. Henderson had caught something in the confluence of the two, something chill and speechless, and he had not.

It wasn't long before the cook came back into himself, ran his blade-nicked hands across his white apron and offered to haul the passenger to his quarters, clean him up. Henderson's voice was low and easy, as always. Neither of them mentioned what had just yawed between them. If they spoke of it, they'd do so after the *McCurdy* had docked and unloaded and the time for stories had come. He left the galley in silence, turning his thoughts to his crew and what he would ask of it. The lifeboats would be frozen hard to their tackle, and the one on the bow might not be there at all. They'd have to go out—on lines or not—and see. And he would go out among them.

Some days later he found himself back in Frieda's kitchen, feeling brow-beaten for reasons that were mucky in his own head. He hadn't been in touch with his sister for almost a month, a fact he registered when he emptied his box at the post office, searching for his pension check and finding letters from charities and colored flyers for the Christmas craft fair. He'd missed the holidays. He stopped at the hardware store and bought his nephews gifts. It would be okay, he thought, to give Frieda money as he usually did. Perfume, a sweater, a scarf—it wouldn't feel right to buy something like that for her. He planned for them to handle each other as they always had, without decoration.

It was the middle of the week, so Frieda put coffee on and allowed him his cigarette, but there was no food. The boys were still at school. The Christmas decorations, which his sister lavished on every surface of her small house, were gone, stored for another year. The brown paper bag that held the unwrapped gifts for his nephews mocked him from the kitchen countertop. A stupid idea. Weak. He smoked in silence, trusting he could hold fast longer than the nervy glimmers of his embarrassment. The boys deserved something. He watched Frieda take things out of the refrigerator and the pantry. She stooped and bent, but even in a sweatshirt and purplish jeans she didn't appear old to him. She was nimble, still concerned with the visitations of failure or success. He was the one who'd aged. He'd run from so many things he'd pretty much run his way to the end of his life.

"You talk to them?"

"Marge and Otto? Oh sure. They were here for—" She shook her head in disbelief. "We all got together for the holidays. Just once, but it was nice. Marge brought the ham, and the girls got along all right with C.J. and Chad. Otto complained about the government, as usual, and the bank, too, if you can believe that. He's on the G. d. board there. I thought Cecil would just bust."

They laughed, both of them, at the vision of Otto preaching about money. Their good brother, so sure of his restraint.

"Sorry I missed the party."

"No, you're not. And I'll tell you again what I told you last year. We've got so we don't miss you. Don't even bring up your name." Frieda was behind him, sweeping the floor. He could hear the hasty, scritching strokes of the broom.

"Makes it easier."

"Yes, it does."

He stood and drifted into the den, into the crabbed and narrow hallway that was so much like the hallways of his youth, drifted into the yellow-tiled bath looking for something to tinker with. When he asked Frieda where he might find replacement screws for the hinges of the clothes hamper, she handed him a shoe box of junk—buttons, paper clips, hardware—and told him to get on with it. He wanted to thank her for taking him up again, but he didn't. He thought about the jaundiced bathroom instead. How his sister never had anything unspoiled or new. He was sorting nails and scrap when his nephews charged into the house, faces stung red from the cold, their cheap, oversized parkas flapping.

They launched into competing stories about teachers and bus brawls before they saw him. C.J., the young one, clammed up at once. Chad dropped his backpack on the table and took up as much space as he could between his uncle and his mom.

"Did you tell him yet?" Chad pinned him with a squint, like he was studying long words on a sign.

"No." Frieda gathered the coats, knocked the slushy boots into a corner. "Hasn't come up."

"Well, I'm bringing it up. Everybody's talking about it."

"Just to be gross," C.J. said, edging out of the room. He was a large-eyed kid, and shy. "You like to think about him under water all winter, down there with the pike and stuff."

"That's enough." Frieda waved an arm as though she was good-humored and tolerant, but he could see the creases around her mouth deepen and how she wouldn't look his way. "Out of here and keep it down. Uncle John and me are talking."

"Then talk to him, will you?" Chad strode into the den. "It's like he lives in the desert or something."

He did a calm inventory in his head. The family was fine—he knew that. Something local, then. A thing spectacular to people who decided to share their tragedies.

"It's just one of those sad messes kids get caught up in because it bothers them. Maybe it'll bother you, too. It was the one you know, Paula's boy. He was running hay out to Mackinac, for the horses there, and the ice broke in a freak way. He's so far down they can't even dive for him. Driving a Sno-Cat. The guys on Ski-Doos are all fine."

He looked at her, reacquainted himself with the wrinkles around her eyes.

"Plain bad luck is what they say. A squall got them off track, and they say one of the snowmobilers—some relative—was drunk, but they didn't do anything stupid. People make that run all the time."

"Been making it for years," he said.

"Yeah," she said, looking at him like she couldn't quite bring his hairline into focus. "Horses have to eat just like the rest of us. Some guy in St. Ignace has the contract, and he let this kid, what's his name, drive the Cat because he asked to. The paper said some nice things."

"Same as dying in a car wreck," he said.

"Maybe so. All the way to the bottom, though, that's different. Feels different to me."

She went on then—to a salting and pounding of meat, stopping once to ask if he wanted to stay for dinner. He didn't. He stood and rinsed his mug, emptied the green-glass ashtray into the trash, found his hat and gloves on top of the refrigerator where he'd left them. Only when he went to put on the gloves did he realize his left fist was clenched. He opened it and saw two wood screws pressed deep into his callused skin, so deep they ought to hurt.

"I'm sorry," his sister said. Her arms were folded tight over her chest, but her face was elongated, soft.

"About what?"

"You know what I mean." And she moved after him to shut the door, sealing her house again from the cold.

When he pulled in across from the Chinook, he realized that his mouth was wet and drooling for a drink while his throat was wrung dry. Divided up, he told himself. Same old story. He went inside, nodded to the men playing eight ball, then slid onto a stool at the bar. He ordered a Coke, and the bartender, a red-haired guy he didn't know, brought it to him right away. He left a good tip and moved to an empty round table against the wall. A stuffed salmon bucked on the wall above him. The air smelled of fry grease and sleep.

He finally thought to slip his coat off so he wouldn't look like he was on the run. Chewed on the ice in his Coke and watched the pool players circle the table like boxers, high-shouldered and flat-faced. He didn't have to wait long. She brought him a second Coke in a highball glass and sat down across from him.

"Hello, John." She'd always said it the same.

"Hello, Paula. Thought I'd come see the sights." He took in her face, which was thinner; he looked for gray in her hair or any bad sign of grief. What he could see right away were diamond-chip earrings and lipstick and the way she hid her hands.

"New jukebox. We got that for big dancers like you. And the kitchen's been redone. You want some food?"

"No," and he shook his head as her wide-set brown eyes smiled. He'd been puke sick in front of her in the old days, there was that humiliation. He'd touched her some as well, as much as she'd allowed from an earnest drunk since she had three or four kids already. That had happened maybe half a dozen times in ten years of drinking, shipping out, moving on. What he'd kept with him most was what hung before him now—her lovely, unassailing face.

"I heard about your boy."

She sat back in her chair and brought a hand up along her neck and ear. Her nails were still short-bitten. "I knew you were here because of that. You remembered, didn't you? That time with the puppy. It's good for me to think of times like that." She began to cry a little, even while she was trying not to, and the tears ran alongside her small, blunt nose. "I didn't see much of Frankie lately. He was living with his father's people. Wanted to do for himself."

He looked down, saw that his distant fingers were shredding a napkin.

"He loved when you sent me home with that crazy pup. Thought it was pure German shepherd and told everybody that, bragging. He was gonna train that dog, too, but it got killed on the road."

All those kids, tangled shapes of her kids, tangle of what she said about them, and him never bothering to sort them out by name or size or worry. No one in the Chinook had. And one of them was Frank, into his life, then out of it like an ass-whipped bad dream. He sat there knowing he'd never given any kid a dog.

"He shouldn't have been on no Sno-Cat. That was plain stupid."

Paula tensed, looked at the wall next to them, then back.

"He was stupid about laying his traps, too. I could have told him if he listened one damn—" He choked up on his loud words as he realized the redheaded bartender was watching him, and Paula was watching, too, but not in the right way.

"You come in here for whiskey, I won't sell you whiskey." She wept openly, with the light of temper rising in her eyes. "Don't talk down my boy, neither. It was a accident. Nobody meant no harm."

"I knew him." He felt terribly hot under his clothes, like he needed to tear them open. "We got along and then we didn't and I tried—"

"Say you're sorry, John. Then move on like we both got to. I'm marrying Pete Norlund." She sniffled and drew her arms tight to her sides. "Frankie hated I was with Pete. And now I don't got that battle to fight."

He took hold of his riptide mind, grappled, and thought about Norlund, a barrel of a Swede older than himself, made rich off timber and real estate. There'd been a stout wife around last he'd heard, but something had clearly been done about her.

"Maybe it'll go good, Paula. You deserve it, if anybody does."

"Still know how to make sweet, do you? I didn't never forget you or the things you did." She stood and covered one of his hands with hers while she reached for his empty glasses. A brush light and warm, but he could feel it go deep just before it left him. Saw her ring, too, set with hard, permanent diamonds. Norlund had a big glassy house on the lakefront. He would work to imagine her in it.

"Sorry about your boy."

She swung her head as if she could fling it empty of tears and walked from him. A black, sleeveless blouse that was more modest than it needed to be. Good boots, tight jeans. Her long, thick hair fanning out from a silver conch clip that he immediately recognized, so like the ones he'd almost brought to her after his trips away, the ones he'd fingered and never bought in those smiling, jostling marketplaces far from home.

He took note of the ragged cuticles of snow left by the plows. Of the snapped-off tree branches. Of the convoyed clouds to the south. There was a way to carry on that every sailor learned after his first few watches—a way to remain alert but separate, never mesmerized or confused by the shape-shifting of fool water or the sky. Peering ahead, looking for decisions to make—that was the way a man remained clear.

He parked on the track, leaving room to swing the canoe out of the shed. He looked her over carefully first, eyeing the seams, checking where he'd patched her in the fall with a square of cloth from a shirt and some amboid glue. She rested cleanly on her braces, a beamy wood-canvas shell. He'd bought her from an old steam tender who'd foul-hooked the end of his luck, gave the man a sluggish Grumman and a hundred dollars in exchange. The steam tender said she came from Minnesota and was made the old-time-trapper way, to last forever. Whatever the truth, she handled well in light water and was easy enough for one man to portage. He slid her off the braces, flipped her, then worked her up on end until he could yoke up between the varnished, seat-worn thwarts. The snow was crusty and deep. It would be a long, panting carry.

By the time he could see the wide silver scuff of the bay he'd begun to sweat through his second shirt.

He took the canoe to the place he always took her, next to a great, smooth log that had washed ashore in a spring storm not long after he'd moved into the shack for good. In summer he chained the canoe along the far side of the log, but he did not chain her now. He merely nestled her into her accustomed place, protected as much from wind and weather as she could be. He was months early. Porcupines or others might do her some mischief, though it was not a possibility that bore thinking about. He'd make up a special buoy before long, get together a good anchor and plenty of strong line so he could mark the spot in the water. What he needed to consider now was when he would next be out there, stroking through the rocky blue shallows of the bay into the lake.

He made his way downshore to a natural cairn of porous, fossil-etched stones, swept them clean of snow, leaned against them. Mackinac Island was a tired mirage beneath the translucent clouds, a smudge of dirtied crystal. Winter had leveled it, as it leveled them all. The boy he'd known had done nothing but take on a few jobs, try on his shifting attitudes. It hurt Paula plenty that he'd died, more than anything had ever hurt him. He knew he wouldn't set foot in the Chinook again, not even to recast his words to her, the ones he'd meant to say better. If he took up liquor, he'd go to the next town to drink it, or drink it in the hidey-hole of his shack as he was expected to.

The sun drifted west until the snow on the lake was shadowed in lavender and blue, and the trees drew themselves into a phalanx of darkness at his back. He had always cared for this, the way the lake sealed itself off, flat and silent and hidden. There was nothing practical to be done about the boy. He could walk the ponds and try to locate the beaver traps, though the uncle would surely come after them before long—maybe he'd come with the girl—and he had no business pretending he was a help to anyone. He was not.

His sweat cooled but did not dry, and there was a chill against his skin. Then the vast hush of an unhindered night brought Henderson back into his mind. Strong, private Henderson who should have been a cook on the lollygagging, sweet-tempered *Pontiac* with its simple runs to Buffalo, but who kept manning the slipshod *McCurdy* in his mind. It had been Henderson who'd done the visceral thing.

He'd run his gang out along the decks, captain's orders, as they needed to know how bad things were with the boats and hatches and rails. Most of them went on safety lines—the decks were slick, the air burned with sleet—but he and Quillian, a true Newfoundland bastard, went footsure and unfettered. They'd discovered the worst, and he was on his way to report to the captain when he saw a man peering at him through a scleric portal. Henderson. Broad and searching in his foul-weather gear, face pressed against the murky glass. He feared the cook wanted to volunteer for his crew, and he did not want that to happen.

He took his tidings to the captain on the bridge. The bosun would need a look at the Number Three hatch; he'd lead him there. There was a kind of march to the whole thing that he relished—a sailor's muster and charge—all done to the drumbeat of weather and damage.

Quillian was waiting for him belowdecks, his face and cap beaded with melting sleet. "The Indian's gone out there. I told him not to." Quillian spoke with neither urgency nor judgment. Narrow talk, the speech of an islander.

"I'll get him. He has some crazy idea about helping."

"Don't know about that," Quillian said. "Had his duffel with him, like he meant to leave."

He pushed his way out then. The deck lights flickered in the thick spray and wind, teasing his sense of balance. He clutched a rail as the *McCurdy* bucked through a shallow trough, water spewing green and black across his face. They'd been spared by the genius of the chief engineer so far, but if she caught beam seas again, caught them hard enough, the decks would be carried under. He looked midships for Henderson, thought again of the blackjacked look in the cook's eyes when the passenger had sworn them off, and made his way down an accursedly icy ladder and aft. Henderson was on the fire crew. Maybe he was crazy enough to take his drill station. If he was still onboard at all.

He found Henderson leaning over a beaten section of railing, sweeping his arms above the frenzied leap of water. Madness. Or an Indian thing, maybe. Or just madness. He'd ask him to come back with him, to the galley for coffee, but if he wouldn't come, so be it. The lake knew her business. He did not move, however, when he saw Henderson lift his duffel—stuffed and heavy—onto the rail. A clumsy shove and the bag went overboard, and while he waited a pitiless moment for Henderson to follow, it did not happen. The cook turned and saw him through the dim shower of spray and nodded, his rain hat tied tight beneath his squarish chin. It was as though he'd known he was being watched. Henderson then passed by and made his way up the ladder with slow purpose. He followed the cook until he met up again with Quillian and the hard-pacing bosun. There were no words exchanged. They all went on with their jobs.

He didn't hear about the passenger until the next day. Awake for thirty hours until the weather broke, out dead for four hours' sleep, then back into the crowded mess for some breakfast. He didn't hear about it from Henderson who was preparing a sherry soufflé for the captain, his apron starched flat, his black hair drawn into a neat, foreign-looking knot at the base of his skull. He heard it from the chief steward who'd been to the passenger's cabin with clean towels and linens. The fellow was gone; the cabin as tidy as a commander's. They were looking for him in every bunk and locker, knowing how panic could make a rat out of any man, but some who'd met him or seen him walking the decks before the storm did not expect to see him again. This was what the steward said, working the tale slowly around his soft Caribbean vowels, savoring it for the drinks a longer, more lush version would someday buy.

He knew. And could feel the knowledge loop about him like a fresh manila line, connecting him hard to Henderson and that damnable yakking man. To Quillian, too, no doubt, though the Newfie would never speak of what he'd seen as he lived ancestrally in the gap between what he witnessed and what he needed to act upon.

Now, standing on a plain of sharded dark and light, at the edge of water and his land, he could not remember what it had been like to look Henderson in the eye after that moment. He could not recall what they'd said to each other, though he knew they must have spoken—each of them—and let the words wrap the shroud on tight. Had they ever gone that far? He knew well how the *McCurdy* had been towed back to Duluth by a Coast Guard vessel with a belligerent crew. He knew Henderson had left the ship, as all the crew did, off to sign onto other freighters while the *McCurdy* underwent repairs. Henderson in his massive pea jacket, his oft-healed hands, a neatly packed duffel like a rolled sail across his shoulder. They had said good-bye to one another in the usual brief way as there were always things left unspoken when a man passed by another man. He remembered that he never questioned Henderson's reasons. The passenger may have died on that pitching galley floor or, good Christ, he may have begged to taste the saltless water of their particular sea. There *had* been a reason, he was sure of it—one that meant everything to the assembled heart that worked inside Henderson.

He walked onto the ice. First to where it laced around the lifeless rocks. Then to where the water of the bay deepened and he could have fished if he cared to, speared his share of whitefish and pike. Beyond, the ice grew thinner and might have groaned and pealed beneath him, but it did not. He went on, to the point where his canoe would begin to feel the draw of the great lake, its deep currents and cold logic. He would plant a hand-painted buoy when the ice broke, pay his delayed respects. The boy was out there, open-eyed and washed and preserved, a victim of risk and channel water, but all he could see were the pitiful man-lights that necklaced Mackinac and adorned her property. He turned back only when the wind rose from the black distance and drove into him, squalling with snow and bitterness. Only when he could be driven ashore like a sail with no good hull or keel beneath him. It was a motion he understood, for it was how his watery heart now worked within him.

ALYSON HAGY grew up on a farm in the Blue Ridge Mountains of Virginia, the daughter of a country doctor, the granddaughter of preachers, blacksmiths, and schoolteachers. She graduated from Williams College and the University of Michigan and is the author of two previous collections, *Madonna on Her Back* and *Hardware River*. A novel, *Keeneland,* will be published by Simon & Schuster in 2000. Forever drawn to weather-whipped places, Hagy is a longtime explorer of the Outer Banks of North Carolina. She currently lives and teaches in Laramie, Wyoming.

Graveyard of the Atlantic was set in Old Style No. 7, essentially a "modernized" version of the classic Caslon types. Its lineage goes back to a face cut in the middle of the nineteenth century by the Miller and Richard Foundry of Edinburgh, Scotland. That face, in turn, engendered another old-style face cut in the United States by the Bruce Foundry in the 1870s. This version was cut by the Linotype Corporation in the 1920s.

This book was designed by Wendy Holdman, set in type by Stanton Publication Services, Inc., and manufactured by Edwards Bros. on acid-free paper.

Graywolf Press is a not-for-profit, independent press. The books we publish include poetry, literary fiction, and cultural criticism. We are less interested in best-sellers than in talented writers who display a freshness of voice coupled with a distinct vision. We believe these are the very qualities essential to shape a vital and diverse culture.

Thankfully, many of our readers feel the same way. They have shown this through their desire to buy books by Graywolf writers; they have told us this themselves through their e-mail notes and at author events; and they have reinforced their commitment by contributing financial support, in small amounts and in large amounts, and joining the "Friends of Graywolf."

If you enjoyed this book and wish to learn more about Graywolf Press, we invite you to ask your bookseller or librarian about further Graywolf titles; or to contact us for a free catalog; or to visit our award-winning web site that features information about our forthcoming books.

We would also like to invite you to consider joining the hundreds of individuals who are already "Friends of Graywolf" by contributing to our membership program. Individual donations of any size are significant to us: they tell us that you believe that the kind of publishing we do *matters*. Our web site gives you many more details about the benefits you will enjoy as a "Friend of Graywolf"; but if you do not have online access, we urge you to contact us for a copy of our membership brochure.

www.graywolfpress.org

Graywolf Press
2402 University Avenue, Suite 203
Saint Paul, MN 55114
Phone: (651) 641-0077
Fax: (651) 641-0036
E-mail: wolves@graywolfpress.org

Other Graywolf titles you might enjoy are:

The Delinquent Virgin by Laura Kalpakian

The Wedding Jester by Steve Stern

How the Dead Live by Alvin Greenberg

A Gravestone Made of Wheat by Will Weaver

Salvation and Other Disasters by Josip Novakovich

The Graywolf Silver Anthology